ROOM
of
MARVELS

"I have just finished reading *Room of Marvels,* and my prevailing thought is, *I hope this is true.* Jim has written a brave book—one that was so honest at times I felt uncomfortable reading it. But that honesty exposes James as being like the rest of us: at times riddled with fear and anger, sin and sadness, but most importantly full of the holy hope of finally going Home. Whatever we imagine heaven to be—and Jim's imagination has run wild in the best way possible—our imaginings won't hold a candle to the grand adventure that awaits us. I challenge anyone to read this book without feeling their stomach flutter with the hope that heaven is as real as it is in our best dreams."

— Andrew Peterson, singer/songwriter

"James Bryan Smith is a vivid storyteller. He takes us—with his character, Tim Hudson—on a marvelous Christian journey, freighted with broad humor and biblical wisdom. This book helps me to remember that the spiritual realm is more real than any other. If you, like Tim, need to slow down and see the splendor of God's design, you will love this book."

— Emilie Griffin, author of *Doors into Prayer: An Invitation*

"One of those profound, special books that only comes along once in awhile, which you're going to want to buy a dozen copies of and give to all your friends . . . . Anyone who is curious about the reality of heaven . . . you simply must read this book."

— *Fuse* Magazine

"There's some serious theology here but communicated in a way that brings it to life, as a story not a commentary . . . . The lessons contained here are needed for all Christians . . . . Highly recommended."

— *Christian Fiction Review*

"Recommend to readers who enjoy allegorical fiction in the tradition of John Bunyan and C. S. Lewis."

— *CBA Marketplace*

"Though I've never lost someone close to me, it will be the first book I reach for when I do."

— *Christian Book Previews*

"A delightful fantasy about one man who visited heaven—reluctantly—and the inspiring lessons he learned."

–Cecil Murphey, co-author of *90 Minutes in Heaven*

ISBN: 978-0-8054-4563-3

Published by B&H Publishing Group
Nashville, Tennessee
www.BHPublishingGroup.com

Interior Illustrations by Aruna Rangarajan

Dewey Decimal Classification: F
Subject Heading: HEAVEN—FICTION
FUTURE LIFE—FICTION

9 10 11 12 13   19 18 17 16 15

ROOM
of
MARVELS

A Story about Heaven that Heals the Heart

JAMES BRYAN SMITH

B&H
PUBLISHING GROUP
NASHVILLE TENNESSEE

Chapter 1

*S*was sitting in my car in a long line at a Massachusetts toll booth. Rain drizzled on my windshield as my car came to a dead stop. I glanced down at the brochure lying on the passenger seat and picked it up with my right hand. "St. Stephen Episcopal Monastery." Below the title was a glossy picture of an old stone building beside a river. "A place to rest, a place to grow spiritually, a place to find stillness. Directed or private retreats available." I wanted to get out of this line and turn back, but I was trapped by the crush of cars inching along. My pastor had given me the brochure a month ago. "You need to take some time away, Tim. You need to deal with your grief," he said. He was right. But the last place I wanted to go was some smoke-and-mirrors religious retreat center.

I glanced at my watch. It was 11:11 A.M. when my old Volvo passed out of the ordinary world, through the stone gateway, and onto the gravel driveway of the monastery.

The stone building looked like a fortress. I passed under the archway entrance, looked back at my car one last time, turned, and kept moving forward. The reception area was completely silent. Wooden paneling covered the walls. The front desk was occupied by a woman with white hair and cat-eye glasses. She looked up from her book and said, "May I help you?"

"Yes, I hope so. I am here for a private retreat. My name is Tim Hudson," I said, reaching out my hand to shake hers.

"Nice to meet you, Mr. Hudson." Her voice was cultivated, with a slight New England accent. "Are you the Tim Hudson who writes books?"

"Well, I have written a few—"

"How lovely to meet you. I've read some of your books. I just finished *God's on Your Side* last week. I enjoyed it very much. My sister in Seattle heard you speak there three years ago, and she gave me one of your books for Christmas last year. Since then I have read them all. It is an honor to have you here. Will you be teaching while you are here?"

"No, I am here for . . . I just need some time to . . ."

"Recharge the spiritual batteries?" she said as she made a small notation on an index card.

"You could say that. Sorry, I didn't catch your name."

"My name is Virginia. It's so nice to meet you. Well, you have certainly come to a beautiful place. Most of the rooms have a lovely view of the river. We have some enchanting gardens, or you can stroll up and down the banks—as long as you stay on the grounds! Which reminds me, if you would give me your car keys, I will have one of the brothers move your car to the lot in the back."

I took my keys out of my pocket and stared at them for a moment before handing them to her.

"It looks like you have requested a five-day silent retreat, is that correct?" she said while placing my keys on a hook behind her desk.

"Yes."

"Very well. The meals are at 8:00 A.M., 12:00, and 5:00 P.M., and everyone is silent except the reader. One of the brothers will be reading from the Bible or from some devotional book. Matins is at 6:30 A.M., morning prayer is at 9:00 A.M., afternoon prayers are at 3:00 P.M., and compline is at 9:00 P.M. Your meeting with your spiritual director is every afternoon at 2:00 with Brother Taylor."

"I am sorry, what did you say?" I asked.

"Your meeting with your spiritual director is—"

"But I didn't request a spiritual director."

"Oh, I know. It is a part of the silent retreat. No extra charge. Of course, you don't have to go, but we highly recommend it. Five days is a long time in solitude. And besides, we all need a little help on our journey now and then."

"I suppose you're right. Right now I just need to rest a bit."

"Your room is number 322. It is up those stairs on your left. Brother Taylor will meet with you in the study, which is room 111, down that hallway."

The stairs, like most of the building, were made of stone. My room—my cell, as they called it—was twelve feet by six feet. "Now I know why they call it a cell," I mumbled to myself as I stood in the doorway. The sparse room consisted of a single bed, a small desk with a wooden chair, and a wardrobe. I put my suitcase down and walked to the window. I lifted up the shade to find myself staring at a brick wall. *Some view,* I thought. *Just my luck—I get to look at a brick wall for five days.* I lay down on the bed in my room without a view and quickly fell asleep.

Without an alarm I awoke at a quarter to two. I ambled down the stairs and through the hallway looking for room III, which was at the very end. I knocked on the door and heard a voice say, "One minute, please." Soon the door opened and before me stood a man in his early forties, not much older than me.

"I am Brother Taylor. C'mon on in. You must be Tim."

"Yes, I am," I said as I walked into a study with all four walls covered with books. "Are all these yours?"

"No, we share this study. These belong to the monastery. We give up all of our possessions when we join."

"Oh, right."

"Have a seat, Tim," he said, pointing to an overstuffed chair. He sat down in a chair across from me.

Even seated, he was an imposing figure. He wasn't tall, but he had the build of a wrestler, and despite his age his hair was thick though gray. *What sort of man,* I wondered, *becomes a monk?* While watching him watching me, I noticed

4

that beneath his cowl he was wearing jogging shoes and sweatpants. He caught my eye as I glanced at the frayed cuffs of his sweatpants, and the corners of his mouth twitched. I realized that he was smiling. I broke the silence when I could not stand it anymore and stammered out the first thing I could think of. "This is a lovely place."

"It is, isn't it?"

It was so quiet I could hear my watch ticking.

"It took me about five hours to get here. I came from Connecticut. I, uh, am a writer."

"Oh really, what kinds of books do you write?" he asked, leaning forward with a curious smile.

"You didn't know I was a writer?"

"No. I'm sorry. Should I?"

"No. I mean, not really. I write spiritual books."

Once again we sat in silence. He was clearly unimpressed that I was a writer. He sat with his hands folded in his lap and continued to stare at me. The silence was unnerving. Finally he asked, "How would you describe your spiritual life right now, Tim?"

"Um, it's OK, I guess. I could use a little rest."

"How would you describe your relationship with God?"

"Gee, isn't that a little personal? Couldn't we talk about the weather for a few minutes before you peer into my soul?"

"I am not sure we have that kind of time."

"I have five days here. I have lots of time."

"Do you?"

"What do you mean?"

"Tim, you must have come here for a reason. People don't usually take five days of their lives to come and stay with us for no reason. Let me ask it another way. What is hurting you?"

"Well," I said, taking a deep breath, "you could say that I have become a hypocrite." I could no longer make eye contact. I stared out the window.

"How so?"

"I am having trouble believing the things I have written."

"What have you written?"

"I wrote a book about how God is *good*. I tell people to turn their lives over to God. I write about how God is fair and merciful and just. It's just . . ."

"Just what?"

"I don't believe it anymore."

"Believe what?"

"That God is . . . good."

"Why is that?"

I looked down at my shoes and took a deep breath.

"Because God is not good," I blurted out. My face instantly flushed with rage.

"Not good?"

I closed my eyes and took another deep breath. My heart began to race. The anger I was about to unleash had been kept deep inside my heart, never spoken to anyone, not even to myself.

"Four years ago my wife and I were so excited when we got the news that she was pregnant with a little girl. We already had a bright, healthy four-year-old boy, and now we were having a girl. I had written some books, and my career seemed to be on the rise. My life could not have been better—a great wife, a great boy, a great career, and now a baby girl. Life was perfect. Then, a few weeks before our daughter was to have been born, the doctor noticed that Rachel had not been gaining weight. She asked for her to have a sonogram, just to make sure everything was all right. During that sonogram they noticed that the baby had a cleft lip and a cluster of other defects. They suspected that the baby had a rare chromosomal disorder and would likely die during her birth. We were told by the doctors to plan her funeral—before she was even born. Can you imagine that? We spent months decorating her room, painting it pink and assembling her crib, and now we were told to be prepared for her to die in the delivery room."

I covered my face with my hands, ashamed of the tears that were now running down my cheeks. Brother Taylor walked to my chair, knelt beside me, and gently put his arm around me.

"I am sorry, Tim." He handed me a tissue and returned to his chair. He closed his eyes, as if he were starting to pray. We sat together for a few minutes in silence. I then took a deep breath and resumed.

"Well, she didn't die. She was born with a number of birth defects, and we did all we could to help her survive.

We flew her to New York for open-heart surgery, which seemed to help. We just kept hoping and praying, asking God for a miracle. She couldn't feed herself, so we fed her through a feeding tube in her stomach. She had around-the-clock medical care from my wife. For the next two years we spent more time in the hospital than at home. We slept on hard floors, and prayed and prayed that God would heal her. She managed to outlive all of the doctors' prognoses—none of them thought she would live to the age of two."

I stopped for a moment and took another deep breath.

"We managed pretty well, despite the fact that our home was filled with medical equipment, and once a month we would have to go back into the hospital for more surgery. When she was just a year and a half we were hit with the second blow. One of my closest friends, a committed Christian who served God far beyond what I have done, was killed in a car accident. He lived in our attic apartment for two years. I loved him like a brother. He was a songwriter, and he had written a beautiful song for our daughter, Madison, because he was so moved by her. He was only forty; he was too young to die. He spent his life giving glory to God and serving the poor, and then he died on the pavement of a rain-soaked highway. How could God have taken him? He was one of the most faithful people I ever met. Countless people were moved by his music. Then suddenly he was gone."

We both sat in silence for a few minutes. I knew the next part would be difficult to tell.

"That's not all. Six months after my friend Wayne died, Madison also died. Catch this—after a routine operation, when she seemed to be fine, she suddenly went into a coma and died within forty-eight hours."

Suddenly the memory of that day flooded my mind. I remembered looking out from the third-floor window of the hospital room. The traffic below flowed on as if nothing had happened. The cars moved and stopped, and pulled into fast-food restaurants or parking lots. People were crossing the street, talking and laughing. I thought, *Don't they know what just happened? How can they not know? How can they go on living as if nothing has happened?* I leaned against the window pane as tears ran from my cheek to the glass and down, like quiet rain.

"Would you like to hold her one last time?" the nurse asked. I sat down in a chair, preparing for someone to hand me my daughter, as I had done a thousand times, but this time would be the last. The nurse offered her lifeless body to me, and I cradled her in my arms. She was still warm. She felt alive, but she was gone from that little body. Forty minutes ago the doctors were trying to keep her alive, applying electric shock to her heart with tiny paddles. We stared at the heart monitor. It stopped and started several times. It was as if she were being pulled away from me but trying to stay. After awhile I could see her body was tired. I leaned in and whispered into her ear, "It's OK, sweet girl, you put up a good fight, you go on with the angels. Daddy will see you soon." My body began to tremble, so much that her bed started to shake. The heart monitor stopped and never came back on.

I felt my pulse quickening from the memory. The anger began to well up in my throat. I stood up and shouted, "Where was God, Brother Taylor? *I* was there! Where was *he?*"

He didn't answer my question. He closed his eyes as if he were praying. I saw a tear forming in the corner of his eye.

"For two years now I've tried to go on as if everything was still OK—you know, 'God's in heaven and all's right in the world,' but just a year after Madison died, my mother died of a heart attack. She was seventy, but she was in good health. She ate right and was active, and suddenly she was gone. She was my North Star. No matter where I was or what I was going through, I could navigate my life because of her. She was my constant in the midst of the chaos. Now that she's gone, I'm completely disoriented. Within three years I've lost my dear friend, my daughter, and my mother—three people who occupy a special place in my heart. I know people die. I know that we are all going to die eventually. It's just . . ."

"Just what, Tim?"

"It's just . . . that it seems so unfair," I finished lamely, knowing I sounded exactly like a discontented schoolboy.

"What's unfair?"

In a rush of anger, my words tumbled out, "I tried hard to please God, to do what is right. I know I am not perfect, not even close, but I am on God's team, for heaven's sake! I am one of God's friends. I mean, I see these horrible parents—drug-addicted, abusive parents—with healthy kids. Why did *we* have to have a child born with some rare disorder? Why, Brother Taylor? Why? Why did my friend Wayne die? Why did my mother die so soon? I am sick of funerals!"

He didn't bother to answer my questions. He simply sat there, looking at me.

"Thank you for sharing that with me, Tim. I will be praying for you. Let's meet again tomorrow."

"What? That's all you have to say? I pour my guts out and you just say, 'See you tomorrow'? C'mon, Brother Taylor, you gotta give me more than that. I am about to abandon my faith. I need your help."

"You need to be silent, Tim, and you have come to the right place. What you need to do is relax and be still for awhile. I want you to let go of your need to be in control."

"Who said I have a need to be in control?"

"Who doesn't, Tim?"

"Well, . . . yeah." We sat there, in silence. Irritated, I shifted position, crossed and uncrossed my arms, and again, feeling a bit like a schoolboy now caught in the principal's office. "But . . ."

"Relax, Tim."

"What am I supposed to do for the next twenty-four hours?"

"Nothing."

"Nothing? My assignment is to do nothing."

"That is precisely what you need to do. Don't do anything that accomplishes something. Take a walk by the river. Sit in the garden. Breathe the air. Slow down. Become present where you are. See you tomorrow, Tim. I will be praying for you. God bless."

Chapter 2

"I HOPE YOU CAN FIND WHATEVER IT IS YOU ARE MISSING."

The cell had not gotten any larger in my absence. Five days in this room was going to be the death of me. I lay down on the bed and fell asleep again. The dinner bell woke me just before 5:00 P.M. I walked to the front desk where Virginia waved to me and pointed to the door where the brothers ate their common meals, called the refectory. There were plates and cups and utensils along the wall and a large pot of soup on a butcher block. A variety of uncooked vegetables rounded out this fine meal. *I will lose five pounds at this place,* I thought. I noticed that all of the monks were thin except one. *He must be sneaking Snickers when no one is looking,* I thought with a twinge of malice. Then I realized that, if I were stuck here, I would probably do the same.

I sat at the silent table and slowly began eating my bean soup and raw carrots. To my surprise, it actually tasted pretty good, kind of like when you are camping and even Spam is something to salivate over. One of the brothers was reading something from the old Scottish writer George MacDonald, as the rest of us quietly slurped and listened. One of the brothers motioned for me to pass the salt, and when I handed it to him, he smiled and nodded. Most of what was read passed over me unattended, but the reader caught my attention with: "Begin to love as God loves, and thy grief will assuage; but for comfort wait His time. What He will do for thee, He only knows. It may be thou wilt never know what He will do, but only what He has done. It was too good for thee to know save by receiving it. The moment thou art capable of it, thine it will be."

Grief, I thought, *does not assuage. Mine has not diminished or healed.* I wondered silently if anyone in the room had suffered through what I had. I glanced at Brother Taylor, sipping his soup. I wondered, *Does he know about disappointment with God? Or has his life been sheltered and cloistered, reading his dusty books and praying five times a day, unaware of the pain outside these walls.*

The silence of the meal was peaceful. It was nice not to have to make conversation, to be clever or seem interested. We just ate. It was strange to do something as intimate as sharing a meal with people but yet not speak to one another. Somehow I felt a sense of belonging even though I had not spoken a word or been spoken to.

I retired to my room and sat there in silence for three hours. Several times I got up and paced the floor like a caged animal. I positioned my chair in front of the window and stared at the bricks. A bell rang, which summoned us to the chapel to participate in what they called "compline," the final service of the day. I didn't feel like praising God or even praying, but I wanted out of my cell. The monks chanted a number of psalms, mixed with some prayers and passages from the New Testament selected for each day of the year. The chapel was more ornate than I, as a Methodist, was used to. After a few minutes I got comfortable with the pageantry. The gold and silver and stained glass, along with the smell of incense, seemed to usher me out of ordinary time and space. The sound of the monks chanting began to move me and made the back of my throat hurt from the ache of unshed tears.

We retired in silence after the service. I went back to my cell. I desperately wanted to speak to someone I knew and loved. I grabbed my cell phone out of my suitcase and went outside.

"Honey, it's me."

"You made it all right?"

"No problem."

"What's it like?"

"It's really pretty here. Kind of medieval in some ways. My room is the size of a closet, the food is meager, and I have a lovely view of a brick wall. But the people seem nice."

"Do you think you can handle five days of silence?"

"I don't know. Jonah survived three days in the belly of a whale, so I suppose I can survive five days in a Massachusetts monastery with a bunch of monks. I know how crazy this all seems. It isn't like me. I mean *me,* at a monastery, hoping, against better judgment, that some-how, somehow—" but I stopped. "Anyway, honey, I really appreciate the fact that you have been so supportive about this whole retreat business."

I heard her sigh, so I tried to lighten the mood. "Oh, and catch this, they assigned me a spiritual director, but I am not too sure about him. He's a jogger."

"What?"

"He's a jogger. I am not kidding. Underneath his cowl he was wearing a pair of jogging pants and running shoes. I was hoping for a chubby old man with a long white beard; instead I got the 'jogging monk.' Imagine that. Me, with a runaway monk. But he seems all right."

"I just hope . . ."

"What?"

"I just hope you can find whatever it is you are missing. It has been hard lately, Tim. Especially watching you suffer. I know you are hurting inside. I hope this helps."

"It will, I think. You are an angel for letting me come here. I don't know if I will find anything while I am here, but there is a good chance I'll lose a few pounds, which won't hurt."

"I like you as you are. I just want you to find your smile again. And come home soon. Nathan and I miss you."

"I miss you guys too. I love you."

"I love you too. Bye."

As I returned to my cell, I saw an older monk with a long white beard coming toward me. He waved and bowed, and I did the same. It figures. There went the white-bearded monk I'd never know. As he walked by me, I saw a glow on his face. When I returned to my room, it seemed even smaller. I sat down at the desk and opened my Bible. Above the desk was a small note, written on a three-by-five-inch card, I hadn't noticed before. It read, "You Are Welcome Here. Enjoy the Solitude. Feel Free to Take Off Your Mask." I decided it was time to quit for the day and try to sleep. I tossed and turned throughout the night. I heard a bell beckoning the monks to matins, the first prayer of the morning. I was too tired to get up and go pray with them, so I stayed in bed. "Pray for me," I whispered, "pray for me." With that I finally fell asleep. When I awoke it was noon, and the lunch bell called us to the refectory where we dined on tuna fish sandwiches and celery sticks.

An hour later I knocked on Brother Taylor's door.

"Good afternoon, Tim."

"Good afternoon, Brother."

We sat in silence once again, and once again I was agitated by it.

"Well, I did nothing, just as you said."

"And?"

"Nothing happened. I am as miserable as I was when I came here. There's nothing to do here. There's no TV in my room, for heaven's sake. I am about to lose it."

"Good."

"Good? How is that good?"

"You're still in control. You're still running the show.

You have to let go. It's like falling asleep, Tim. You can't make yourself fall asleep, no matter how hard you try. At some point you just let go."

We sat in silence again.

"Speaking of sleep, tell me about your dreams, Tim."

"Are you some kind of dream therapist?" I asked. He shook his head no. "Well, lately they have been nightmares."

"Could you tell me about them? Do you have any that you can remember?"

"Well, for the past few months I have had this same dream. Man, I have never told this to anyone. Oh well, here goes. In this dream I am wandering through a field at night during a thunderstorm. The only shelter I can find is an old abandoned house. I go inside the house and discover that it is a morgue. I open up a door, and there is a creepy old man standing over a workbench with his back to me. He is laughing in a sinister way while he chisels on a stone. I look over his shoulder to see what he is chiseling, but I can't quite see what he is doing because it is too dark. Then lightning flashes, and I suddenly see that he is chiseling names on tombstones. There are four tombstones in front of him, and they bear the names of the three people I have lost, Madison, Wayne, and my mother, Rose. He is carving another name on the fourth one, but I wake up before I see whose it is."

Brother Taylor stared out the window, seemingly lost in thought.

"Pretty creepy, huh?"

"It is certainly not pleasant."

"Sounds like I'm a candidate for some major therapy, don't you think?"

Brother Taylor smiled.

"So, what do you think it means?"

"I think it means you are a person in need of better dreams."

I smiled back at him.

"Tim, do you believe in heaven?"

"Of course. I am Christian."

"I mean *really* believe it. Do you have a strong sense of certainty that the people you lost are doing well?"

"I do. I mean, intellectually I do. But I don't have any proof. I would like to believe there is a heaven. But sometimes I think it might be just wishful thinking. My dad used to say that when people die, they die. Game over. Just like an ant or an amoeba or a mountain goat. We die and we cease to exist."

"Do you think he's right?"

"Well, not really. I can't believe that when we die it just ends. I like the idea of heaven. But in a sense I am no better off than my father. Neither of us has any proof."

Another long silence passed between us. I thought about my nightmares and prayed silently that they would somehow pass. The clouds must have parted because sunlight suddenly penetrated the room. I could see the dust on top of the books. I hung my head, with my chin pressing into my chest.

"Tell me about your prayer life, Tim."

"There's not much to tell. I don't pray much anymore."

"Why?"

"There was a time when I prayed. I used to believe that prayer made a difference. But then I prayed to God in my deepest time of need. I begged God to heal our daughter, and he didn't hear me. I haven't prayed since."

"How do you know that God didn't hear you?"

"He didn't give me what I asked for, even though I prayed it as hard as anything I have ever asked of him. My faith was hanging on that prayer."

"In your judgment, then, God did not hear you because he didn't answer your prayer. Is that what you think?"

"Sure."

"Is there a chance that God knew better?"

"Look, all I know is that I am worse off because of God's refusal. I would have believed in him if he had heard my prayer and answered it."

"Until the next desire came along."

"What is that supposed to mean?"

Brother Taylor tilted his head and smiled at me. His eyes softened, and he said, "You would have continued to believe in God until the next desire came along that God would not grant. You would have turned him away then. With your arrangement it would only be a matter of time."

"That's easy for you to say. Have you ever buried a child?"

"No," he said, averting his eyes from mine.

"Have you ever suffered through something and asked God to help, only to have him . . . seem to look the other way?"

"Yes I have, Tim."

"What? What was it? Tell me about it?" I asked.

He sat in silence, looking at the bookshelf. He shifted uncomfortably in his chair, leaning forward, while pressing the tips of his fingers across his lips, as if wanting to tell a secret and yet shushing himself.

"This is not about me; it is about you. I am sorry for presuming. But you can trust me when I say that I have been through . . . let's just say I know about unanswered prayer. What I was trying to say is this: When God hears our prayers, he sees more than his children at the moment of their prayer. He sees the eternal effects of our prayers. To give us what we want because we want it would be to put our fate in our own hands. If God did that, he would not be God. He would be more like the devil."

I sat and thought about what he was saying. He had exposed my childish way of thinking. "Forgive me for being preachy," he said.

"No need to ask for forgiveness. Right now I need a little preaching, I think. What do you mean by 'the eternal effects of our prayers'?"

"God knows better than we do. He sees more than we can see. So he doesn't deal with us as a child of today but as a child of eternal ages. So God listens, hears, considers, and deals with our requests out of the perfect tenderness of his heart. That is enough for me. When I realize that, I am not concerned that I don't get what I ask for. I trust that God has something better in mind for me, even if I can't see it yet."

The clouds blocked the sun and the room darkened. I nodded in agreement with what he was teaching me.

"So, what do I do now? I am not sure I am ready to pray," I said.

"That's all right. But there is something I would like you to do for the rest of the day. Read and reflect on a passage of the Bible. Luke 1:26–38."

"Only one passage? I can do more than that. I have a lot of time and no television."

"That one passage will be plenty. There is a lot to reflect on in that story. Pay attention to the words. Listen to it with your heart. Enter into the story. Feel the words; don't just try to understand them."

"I'll do my best. See you tomorrow."

"Sweet dreams, Tim," he said as he shook my hand.

With that I left the study and went back to my cell. I opened my Bible to the passage he had assigned and began to read. It was the story of when the angel Gabriel came to Mary to tell her that she would bear a child. Mary questions how this can be since she is a virgin. The angel tells her, "'For nothing will be impossible with God.' Then Mary said, 'Here am I, the servant of the Lord; let it be with me according to your word.' Then the angel departed from her."

I was struck by those words: "Let it be with me according to your word." I wondered how Mary, just a young girl, could have trusted God enough to utter those famous words, "*Let it be.*" I stayed in my room the rest of the afternoon. The dinner bell rang, but I didn't feel like eating, so I sat there, staring at the brick wall outside my window. An hour later there was a knock on my door. I opened it, and the older monk was standing there holding a tray of food. Rachel would be amused that I was under the care of the white-bearded monk after all. He handed it to me, smiled and bowed, and walked away.

After eating a few bites, I put on my old blue pajamas and lay down on my bed, feeling as desperate and alone as I have ever felt. I wanted to go home, to see Rachel and Nathan. It was too late to leave. I lay in bed staring at the ceiling, trying to fall asleep. "Speak to me, God. Please. Speak to me. I think I need an angel right now. Speak to me. Please. . . ."

Chapter 3

When I awoke, I found myself in a darkened, empty train, with no idea where it was headed. Inside the train was pitch black. The only light was something like moonlight outside the windows. The darkness seemed to be diminishing by the second. Off in the far horizon was a faint streak of peach in the sky, indicating that there was light ahead. It was as if the train was heading into a sunrise.

When there was sufficient light, I noticed a black sweater lying on the seat in front of me. It was one of those old Irish fishermen's sweaters. I was feeling a little chilly, so I decided to put it on. It fit perfectly. Without any warning the train came to a halt. I got out and walked on the platform. There were no signs. No one seemed to be driving the train. I had no idea where I was.

A path leading away from the platform seemed to head into the woods. A single lamppost stood just off the platform. The ground was covered with leaves—brown, yellow, red, and orange. The sweet odor of decay was in the air. *It must be autumn in this place,* I thought. Not knowing what else to do, I started walking down the path. The path ended at the bottom of a hill. I turned in circles, wondering which way to go. I lifted up my eyes toward the small hill whose shoulders glowed.

The rays of the light seemed to be calling me over that hill. I walked up to its peak, and I could see a cottage a hundred yards away, and through a large window I could see a fire burning. The sight of the fire strengthened me against the cold as I walked down the path toward it. It suddenly occurred to me that I was sleepwalking in the woods in my blue pajamas and someone's black wool sweater. At that point I figured it must be a dream so I might as well enjoy it.

Lining each side of the path were white lilies, taller than normal. Every lily was glowing with a light of its own, an internal light that emanated from its core. The light was similar to a street lamp, only strong enough to light the area around it. When I touched one of the blossoms, it felt as if the petals were made of iron, yet each moved at my touch. I walked down the path feeling a little frightened. "It's just a dream," I muttered to myself, and with that new thought I picked up my pace toward the cottage.

The path, and the lilies, came to an end about a hundred feet from the cottage. As soon as I stepped off the path, I was surrounded by a pack of wolves—I counted seven—looking ravenous. Our eyes met, and I froze in fear. My feet felt like they were attached to the ground; I couldn't move. My heart began to race with the thought that I might not be dreaming at all. I wanted to turn and run but couldn't. The wolves moved closer. Then suddenly a lion appeared from the woods. He let out a roar and sent the wolves running away, howling as they fled. The lion glanced back at me and then began walking toward me. Sweat was trickling down my sides. Though the lion was three times my size, I was somehow not frightened by him at all.

The lion walked back toward me until he got right up in my face, so close I could feel his breath. He looked at me with a look that said, "Do not be afraid." He walked behind me, forced his head between my legs, and flipped me up on his back. I was suddenly riding on the back of a large lion, seated between his shoulders and holding onto his mane.

The lion walked up to the front door of the cottage and stopped. He put his chin to the ground, and I slid over his neck, left standing on the doorstep of the cottage. The lion quickly padded off into the woods without a sound. I turned back to the door in front of me and started to knock when it opened by itself, making my knuckles hit nothing but air. It was chilly outside, and the fire looked inviting.

The cottage was small and mostly bare, consisting of one large room. The fire was still burning in the fireplace, the kind whose coals glow at the base. There was only one chair in the whole room. It was an old-fashioned barber's chair. The fireplace had a white mantel with nothing on it but a single candle that seemed to give enough light to illumine the whole room. I began to wonder what time it was and where in the world I was. I looked down at my watch. The second hand wasn't moving.

There was nothing on any of the walls except one picture, a framed photo, above the mantle. As I got closer, I noticed that there was a person in the photograph, a small boy sitting in a sandbox with his sand pail and a shovel, laughing at nothing in particular, it seemed, just laughing because he was having fun. Just as when a person near you yawns it makes you yawn, so the laughter coming from this picture made me begin to smile, even though I had no idea what he was laughing about or why. I inched closer to see it more clearly.

"Oh wow," I blurted out. "It's me."

It was a framed photo of me as a small boy, but it was one I had never seen before, one that obviously did not make it into the family albums. I would have remembered this one. I vaguely remembered the day, and I remembered the sandbox, but I could not recall Mom or Dad or anyone ever taking a picture of me in it. The more I tried to figure out the mystery of the photo, the less at ease I felt in this strange but peaceful cottage.

"It's a great picture," a voice said from behind me.

Startled, I turned around to see who it was. It was an older man wearing a white coat. He appeared to be in his sixties, with only a wisp of gray hair on his plump but pleasant head. He wore gray flannel pants and well-worn wing-tip shoes. In one hand he was holding a pair of scissors and in the other a black comb. As soon as I noticed the scissors and comb, I recognized who he was.

"Ernie?" I said.

"Yesiree. How are you, Tim? You look a little tired."

"Ernie . . . I haven't seen you in—"

"A long time."

"Ernie, what are you doing here? You died—"

"About twenty years ago in your time. But it seems like only a moment ago to me. You know what they say about how time flies. Well, yesiree, I did die, yes, I sure did. Well, I really didn't die. I just left the place where you live."

I interrupted this time: "Speaking of which, where exactly am I?"

"You're in your Father's house . . . *our* Father's house, that is. Yesiree."

"How did I . . . get here?"

"Well," Ernie said, with a huge and growing grin, "you finally got to that blessed place—God's address."

"God's address? Where's that?"

"At the end of yourself!" Ernie laughed.

"At the end of myself?"

"Yesiree. The place of complete desperation. It happened when you were asking for help."

"I don't remember asking for help."

"You said you needed help. So God rallied the angels, and we all began to stir."

"Who began to stir?"

"Lots of people."

"But, Ernie, I wasn't really praying. I was just falling asleep. I fell asleep while I was praying! That's hardly a spiritual feat."

"Yeah, God has a sense of humor. Just when you surrendered, he brought you here. That's when he does some of his best work. That's because it's all by grace. You've been rejecting him, but now you find yourself in the place you always wanted to be. Here. In your Father's house."

I was utterly speechless. A few minutes ago I was trying to fall asleep in an uncomfortable bed, and now I am here with my dead barber, who is not actually dead at all. In fact, I never saw Ernie look better. He doesn't even have his usual bad breath—one of the many reasons I hated getting haircuts throughout my childhood.

Ernie was always nice, though. He gave me my very first haircut. My mom stood by the chair and held my hand because I was so scared. I tried to act brave. When it was over, he gave me a lollipop, a kind of reward for enduring being Samsonized. I remembered how his combs seemed to dance in the blue water, floating up and down in the sterilizing jar. And the final act of each cut—shaving my neck with a straightedge razor—always gave me goose bumps.

"What are you doing here, Ernie? I mean, if this is God's house, where is God?"

"Oh well, Tim, you can't see God," he said with a sad and serious look. "You aren't dead yet. You're still seein' through the glass dimly."

"I see—no pun intended. Have *you* seen God, Ernie?"

"Oh yes. Yes, yes, yes, I have! I have seen him many times. Yesiree. It's a wonderful thing, I can promise ya that."

"Then I can assume that when you died you went to heaven . . . assuming this is heaven."

"You sure can."

"Well, I have to confess, Ernie. I didn't know you were a Christian."

"Well, I didn't talk about my faith. I just tried to live it. I didn't preach to my customers. Maybe I should have. But I prayed for 'em. Every one of 'em. Even mean old Mr. Alexander. He was pretty bald, so it meant for a short prayer! But seriously, I decided one day to try to be the kind of barber Jesus would have been if he had been in my wing tips."

"You were always kind to me, Ernie. I remember that. But why are you here with me . . . now?"

"Because God chose me."

"Chose you . . . why?"

Ernie looked at me and only smiled.

Then it hit me.

"Aw, I get it. You prayed for *me,* didn't you?"

"Yesiree. I said I prayed for all of my customers, and that includes you."

"Yeah, but I was just a little boy."

"Yep, you were, and a scared one at that. Your mama had to hold your hand while I cut. I used to pray for you to calm down and not be afraid. And then I would pray that one day the Lord would reveal himself to you. I said, 'Lord, bless this fine young boy. Let him know how much you love him. One day, Lord, make him into something special.' Remember when I used to tilt your head forward so I could cut the back? That was when I laid my hand on you and prayed for you."

"Wow, I never knew that."

"Of course not. I didn't pray out loud. I did it secretly, like Jesus said. Even my scissors hand didn't know what my comb hand was up to!"

"Thanks. Thanks for doing that," I said as I turned my eyes to the ground. Whenever I hear that someone has prayed for me, I feel embarrassed and cannot find words to thank them.

"Ernie," I said softly, "I did become a Christian but not till I was eighteen."

"Well, prayin' ain't like gettin' somethin' from a vending machine. It ain't automatic. We just pray and let God figure out how and where and when."

"Yeah. I guess so. Thanks. But I . . . have sort of lost my—"

"I know, I know, Tim," he said, with a look that told me I needed to say no more.

My eyes drifted back to the fireplace and, more particularly, to the picture above the mantle.

"Ernie, tell me about this picture on the wall. What's it doing here?" I asked.

"That's a picture of you, Tim. It's one of God's favorites," Ernie replied.

"But I don't remember it being taken."

"It wasn't. At least not by a camera. It's one of God's memories. He put it here on the wall because it is one of his favorites, like I said. And he wanted you to see it."

"Boy, I look so happy," I said as I looked closer at the face of the young boy laughing toward the sky. It is so strange to look at photos of yourself as a child. I stared in wonder at the person I once was, and I was wishing I could return to those days of innocence.

"Nope, you can't," Ernie said.

"Can't what?"

"You can't return to those days of innocence, but you can see the world with different eyes."

"What? . . . How did you? . . . Can you read my mind?" I asked.

"Sure I can. Up here there are no secrets." I stood silent for a few moments, stunned.

"Yep," Ernie said, breaking the silence, "There's nothing he likes more than when his creation rejoices. You've lost your joy, Tim. He wants you to find it again."

"How is he going to do that? How is he going to restore my joy?"

"You'll see soon enough. How about a haircut?"

"Do I really need one?"

"You look a little shaggy to me."

I remembered that anything longer than a buzz cut seemed too long to Ernie. The sixties and seventies were not easy for Ernie in this regard. He smiled and held up his scissors and comb. I could not help but say yes.

I sat down in the old-fashioned barber's chair. "I don't need a booster seat anymore, Ernie," I said. He threw the black cape around me, placed the white tissue paper around my neck, tightened the cape with the snap, and began to pump the seat up with his foot.

"Looks like you've lost a little on top, Tim."

"A little? How about a lot? Male-patterned baldness is not the joy it is cracked up to be."

"Well, like I always said, 'Hair today, gone tomorrow.'" Ernie said, laughing at his own joke. "Besides it just means God has less to do."

"Less to do?" I asked, playing along with what I sensed would be another bad joke.

"Yesiree. The Bible says God knows the number of every hair on our heads. So in your case he has fewer to count!"

Biblical barber humor is a rare find, and though hair-loss jokes wore thin a few years ago, I played along, and we both smiled for awhile as he continued to cut what hair I still have.

"So you told me *how* I got here. The end of myself and all. But you haven't told me *why?* Why am I here?"

"I already told you, remember? He wants to restore your joy. There's a lot inside of you that's hurtin'. You've had some real losses, and you've beaten yourself up pretty good tryin' to figure it out. He heard your prayers, and this is his answer."

"I don't remember praying for . . . this."

"I didn't say the prayers you said with your lips. Those are fine and all, but the ones God really pays attention to are the silent ones. The ones that come from so deep in your heart words can't express 'em."

"But how will this place . . . restore my joy?"

"All in good time, Tim, all in good time. He brought you here to show you some things. You just be still awhile, and I'll finish this haircut."

As Ernie clipped away, I settled into the chair, closed my eyes, and took a deep breath. The cottage was so peaceful. A sense of being loved began to well up from deep inside me, like when you come home after you have been away awhile and everyone is so happy to see you.

"How ya feelin' now?"

"I feel fine. Really fine."

That was an understatement. This cottage radiated with warmth and acceptance, that honest kind of welcome, the "I know you've made a mess; I know all of your broken promises and your shameful moments and your worst thoughts—but you are still welcome here" kind of acceptance. Ernie broke my train of thought by sticking a mirror in my face. "What do you think?"

I looked at my own reflection and felt a shudder in my soul. Ernie brought the mirror in closer. It is shocking sometimes to look deeply into your own eyes.

"Look deeper, Tim."

My vision blurred for a moment. The face I saw looked different. *Dear God,* I thought as I looked at the face I had not really wanted to look at for years, *look at how sad I am. And how tired.*

I saw a tear form a ring around my left eye, then pool and run down my cheek.

"A face that could move the very heart of God!" a voice said from behind us, a deep voice with a British accent.

"Hello, Jack," Ernie said. "I thought you might be the one. It's good to see you! Come on in!"

Chapter 4

"Look a little harder, Tim."

$\mathcal{A}$ large man moved into the light and reached his hand out to shake mine. He had a jolly face and a pleasant, almost mischievous, smile. He was wearing an old, tattered tweed suit. He looked a little like someone I had seen pictures of, but he was glowing so much I could hardly define his features. The light coming from him was so bright at first I shielded my eyes. He turned his face to me and smiled, and for a moment I thought I knew who he was.

"Are you?"

"Please, stay seated," the man in the suit said.

"It's an honor to meet you, Mr. . . . You are . . . *him*, aren't you?"

"Please, call me Jack. I suspect we are going to spend a good deal of time together." He looked frumpy yet wise. Joy seemed to emanate from his face.

"Now," Jack said, "let's talk about the man in the mirror, shall we?"

Trembling, I said, "I would rather talk about you, I mean, if you are him. Your writings changed my life. I—"

"I am not here to be flattered. I am here to serve. In fact, now that I have crossed over, I can truly say that flattery will get you nowhere! I am here to be your guide."

"My guide? To where?"

"Ernie already told you, I suspect. You are in your Father's house. And there are many, many rooms. And there is a special room, just for you, a room of marvels, where you have been invited to go. I was asked to be your guide. Right now you are in a kind of welcoming room, but your ultimate destiny is much greater."

"Again, forgive me, but are you . . . C. S. Lewis, the famous author?"

"No."

"But, you . . . you look, I mean, you seem like him, or, what I imagine him to be."

"Up here we go by our real name. I suspect you read about that in your Bible. Revelation 2:17: 'To everyone who conquers I will give a white stone, and on the white stone is written a new name that no one knows except the one who receives it.' So you see, my real name, well, only God and I know. But please, call me Jack, Mr. Hudson."

"Only if you call me Tim."

"Very well, Tim. Now take a look in that mirror and tell me what you see."

A long silence passed between the three of us. Ernie stood holding the mirror. It was no ordinary mirror. It did not merely reflect physical features; it reflected the condition of one's soul. In that mirror I saw myself as I truly am, not the self I want others to see, or even the person I try to convince myself I am. I saw my true self. My sinfulness, my weaknesses, my evil thoughts were revealed. I pulled back in horror.

"I can't look at it!"

"I know it is hard, Tim, but please look again."

I turned to look into the mirror. I could see my sad face looking back at me. I looked into my own eyes, and all I could feel was despair. "I'd rather not, Jack."

"Why?"

"Shame," Ernie interjected. "Isn't that so, Tim?"

"Shame is too mild. I hate what I see. I am a mess. I am a fake. I am a hypocrite. I know the depths of my own depravity. I know the hundreds of resolutions I have broken. I know who I am. If you knew all of the sins I have committed, you would not be standing near me."

"Oh," said Jack, "but we do, and are! A man is more than the sum of his sins. Look a little harder, Tim."

I took a deep breath and peered into the mirror. At first I only saw my own hideous reflection, but then, like those line drawings that, when your eyes relax, reveal something you could not see before, something emerged. It was me, really me. Not a two-dimensional portrait, or a three-dimensional reflection, but a multidimensional exposure. I saw my true self in that mirror. Flawed, broken, wounded, and imperfect, but real.

"Nothing—no one, is more beautiful than you, Tim, since God, beauty itself, has fallen in love with you," Jack said.

"What about . . ."

"Your sins?" Ernie asked.

"Yeah. I mean, what about them? Isn't there a big black book up here, where they keep all of the records? My book must be several volumes."

"Yes, there is a record," Jack said, "and their effects written in our souls. We weren't made for sin. It damages us. Your sins can be seen by the effect they have had upon you. But up here it all changes."

I continued to stare into the mirror until I began to sob. Ernie and Jack each put a hand on my shoulders and gently rubbed my back.

"You *are* forgiven, Tim. He died for *all* of your sins, not some of them. God loves you. All of the time," Ernie said.

God loves me. This was not a new thought; it was an old thought I had long ago abandoned, especially in the last year. I had lived for years believing that there is something I must do, something I must be, in order to get God to like me. When bad things began happening to me, I was sure that God was punishing me. After Madison's birth there were many times of introspection where I asked myself, "What did I do wrong? If I had only been a better Christian!" As I sat in the chair, I thought, how comically tragic, that all of my efforts to be loved were a waste of time and energy. Jack and Ernie continued to massage my shoulders, and it felt like the heavy weight that had been pressing on my back was lifted.

I whispered these words, "I am sorry . . . thank you," and when I did, the room was brighter than it had ever been. In fact, it was as if the sun had just come over the horizon. Jack pointed to a door I had not noticed before and motioned me toward it.

"You are ready to go through it now. The door would not have opened for you before. Now that you know who you are, and whose you are, you are ready for your journey."

Chapter 5

*W*hen we walked through the door, I was once again outside, but it was no longer dark. It was more like early morning, when the rooster crows because the sun has just appeared. I was struck by the utter stillness of the place. Though it was full of life—birds singing and insects humming—it was an entirely peaceful sound. The trees were large and beautiful, like they were people, each with a different look about them, as if they wanted to say something to me.

I was also struck by the vastness of the place. It was a larger sort of space, as if the sky were farther off than I remembered ever seeing it on Earth. I had the sense that I was, for the first time in my life, truly "outside," in a place much larger even than our solar system. I felt liberated and yet exposed at the same time.

It was not yet light, but the whole sky was beginning to glow. The light was coming from the distant horizon, as if there were a sun just below it. The beams were not yellow or even white but rosy as they lit the clouds above us. The air smelled rich with life, like a forest after the rain. Jack motioned me to walk with him. We began hiking up a trail that led through the woods that surrounded the cottage.

Now that we were out in the light, I could see Jack more clearly. He looked very different than he did in the room. The best way to describe it is to say he looked a bit like a hologram because when I looked at him from different angles, I saw different dimensions. From one perspective he looked like a jolly Father Christmas, but from another angle I could see he was like a shining Olympian rippling with power, as if he were hiding himself from me so as not to frighten me with his glory. The path was on a gentle incline, but I was soon growing tired. Within a few steps I found that I couldn't go on. I stopped in my tracks as my breathing became labored.

"Having a bit of trouble?" Jack inquired.

"Yes, I . . . can't catch my breath. How is it that I . . . who am relatively young . . . can't stay up . . . with a dead guy?"

"Hardly dead. I am more alive than ever! Let's rest awhile."

We sat down on a nearby rock. He looked around and smiled. I was still catching my breath. There was a nice moment of silence. Then my thoughts turned back to Ernie's mirror. A deep sense of shame returned to me once again as I recalled how many sins I had committed. The envy, the anger, the lust, the gossip, the hate, the prejudice, and the pride—and those were just the sins of commission; the sins of omission were even more troubling. It was too much to think about. But I did think about it, and as I did, I became more and more ashamed.

"I can't go on, Jack."

"Why not?"

"Because I am not worthy to be here. I need to go home and . . . change my ways or something. The things I have done and left undone—it's too much," I said.

"Self-improvement is not the way to heaven. If you were to go back and try to change, it would only be to try to earn something, to once again put yourself in control. Here's the good news—you are not in control!"

"Jack, I am not good enough to be here—to be in this place, to be here with you. I am not worthy . . . to be! I have made a mess of it all. God gave me enormous gifts, and I squandered them. I am wretched! After what I have seen here, I can't even bear to look at this place."

"Let me ask a simple question. Who made your eyes?"

"What? That is something a two-year-old would ask?"

"Who made your eyes?"

"God? Is that what you are looking for?"

"Precisely. It was God, and he wants you to use them to see his marvels."

"But, Jack, you don't understand. You haven't seen what I have done with these eyes. Instead of beauty all I see are terrible things. It is as if I have ruined them. I haven't used them to see his glory. Please, Jack, let me go where I deserve."

"Yes, it is right to feel shame. Judging is a part of loving, and back in that room you were able to see who you are. But that mirror does not get the last word. I have something special I want you to see, Tim. Come with me."

He pointed to the summit of the hill.

"Let us walk a bit," he said. "Lean on my arm, and I will strengthen you."

Jack's strong arm supported me as we ascended. We walked up to the top of the hill, and there stood a cross. My body began to tremble as I realized that I might be looking at the actual cross upon which Jesus had been crucified. I let go of Jack's arm and ran to the foot of the cross and fell to my knees. I ran my hands up the rough wood and gazed upon the blood stains that ran down toward me. I hugged the wood and blubbered like a baby.

"I am so sorry, Lord, . . . so sorry," I said as I kissed the blood-stained wood.

"He bore the blame and took away your shame, Tim. Isn't it wonderful!" Jack said from behind me.

I looked up at the blood stains on the cross piece where his hands had been pierced.

"There was not, nor will be," Jack said, "from the first day to the last night, an act so glorious and magnificent."

I stood up full of courage. "I am ready to serve him with all of my heart," I said.

"That is not why he died for you, Tim. He doesn't need

your service. He died for you because he loves you. He doesn't need you to do anything at all. Now you are faced with a more difficult task: to let him love you in the midst of your shame. He did not die to coerce you into service or into moral improvement. All he wants . . . is you." I stared in silence at the blood-stained wood.

"You must let him love you as you are, not as you intend to be. Let him love you as you are, without a single plea for reform. It is all about grace, Tim. All of life is grace. We deserve nothing; we are given everything. Until now you have only experienced the drippings of grace. You have longed for the real thing, like the longing for the scent of a flower you have never been able to find, or the echo of a tune you have not yet heard, or news from a country you have never visited. Well, now you have found it. Grace is the thing you have been searching for, and it is all around you."

"I thought you might be needing this again," said a voice from behind us. It was Ernie, standing by Jack, holding the same mirror. He handed it to Jack, who walked to my side and put it in front of me again.

"Now, look again at the man in the mirror."

I wanted to look away, but he held it there, refusing to let me escape the face in front of me. As I looked this time, a new feeling came over me. It was the first time in my life I had ever really looked at myself without contempt.

"Jesus called us to love the least of the brethren," Ernie interrupted. "It appears to me that right now the least of the brethren . . . is you. Do you think you could love yourself for his sake?"

I just kept looking at the face. In my own eyes I could see a thousand failures, countless hurts and losses. I looked up at Jack and Ernie in confusion. I was no longer angry with the man in the mirror. I felt pity more than anything else.

"God has forgiven you, Tim. Now you must forgive yourself, unless you think you are a higher judge than God," Jack said. "If he has forgiven you, who are you not to forgive yourself?"

I looked again into the mirror and could see Ernie's smiling reflection. I focused again on my face, took a deep breath, and said softly, "I forgive you."

Jack and Ernie helped me to my feet, and together we walked down the other side of the hill. There were scores of angels surrounding the path, bright and shining and brimming with radiant power.

"What are they doing here?" I asked.

"Angels do not understand mercy. They marvel at it. They often wonder why God bothers with us humans. But every now and then they see an act of love or mercy or forgiveness, and they stand in awe. What you just did—forgiving yourself despite your failures—is something that amazes them," Ernie explained. As I walked by them, the angels covered their faces so their shining glory would not blind me.

When we reached the bottom, there was a fork in the path, and Ernie turned to us and said, "Well, boys, I think my work here is done. Tim, it has been a pleasure you cannot imagine. Jack, a joy as always. Good-bye."

We hugged, and then Ernie turned and walked away, and I watched in amazement as my old, dead-but-alive barber ambled along, laughing and waving his scissors and comb in the air.

"Now you have seen with the eyes of God. You have seen yourself as God sees you: a sinner who is nonetheless loved," Jack said as we walked along our path, putting his arm around me and hugging me as if I had just hit the game-winning home run.

"Am I ready to see this room you have been talking about?"

"Not yet. There is more to see before you get there."

Chapter 6

"Do you know why I am angry with God?"

We continued to walk down a path that led into a deep, green, lush forest, with shafts of light penetrating through to the ground. We walked in silence for a few hundred yards.

"This is a little like Dante, isn't it?" I asked.

"How do you mean," Jack asked.

"If I remember right, *The Divine Comedy* begins, 'Midway in my life's journey, I went astray,' right? Dante hit his midlife, and I suppose so have I. So in his dream he gets to see the afterlife to help him understand his life on Earth. I am forty, and it appears I have gone astray. He went on a journey to see things that would help him understand the big picture, and Virgil was his guide. Is that what is going on here? You won't tell me your real name, but I can ask this: are you my Virgil?"

"Egad! Virgil? Me? No! Incidentally, it was Beatrice, and not Virgil, who guided Dante through heaven, and I am no

Beatrice, as you can see! And second, thankfully, we didn't have to start in hell!"

We both started laughing. Hearing Jack laugh confirmed what I had always suspected; the true sign of sanctity is not seriousness but joy.

"I was wondering, Jack, when will I be ready to see this room?"

"Oh, I wish I could take you there now, but you are not yet ready. Fortunately, you have taken the first step out of your fool's paradise. You know who you are, and you have forgiven yourself. But there is someone else you need to forgive."

"Who?"

"You will see soon enough. You are here because God is gracious. You have a chance, like Dante—or even," and here he smiled, "Charles Dickens's Scrooge—to see things that will change your perspective and, ultimately, the way you live when you return. Do you remember what Nathan said to you when you tucked him in one night, a few weeks ago?"

"No."

"It was about the Lord's Prayer."

"Oh yes, I remember. I was explaining to him what it means for us to pray, 'Forgive us our trespasses.' I said to him, 'It means that we are to forgive each other as God forgives us.' Then, he asked, 'What about God? Who forgives God, Dad?'"

"And how did that make you feel, Tim?" Jack looked straight into my eyes.

"I remember that my heart sank."

"Why?"

"Because I knew . . ."

"Knew what?"

"I knew that I had not . . . forgiven God."

"Precisely. And that is what you must learn to do. You have not forgiven God."

"But God doesn't need to be forgiven—God never sins."

"Of course God never sins, and in that sense we do not need to forgive him. But that does not prevent us from being angry with what he does, or more precisely, what he *allows*. The psalms are full of people being angry with God, questioning what God has done. There is nothing wrong with being honest with God. But your anger is misplaced. There is much for you to see and much for you to know. Perhaps then you will be able to let go of your anger."

"But, Jack, do you know why I am angry with God?"

"Of course I do. In the past few years you have lost a close friend, a young child, and your mother—all taken too soon in your estimation. And you have been thinking, *I have tried hard to live as a Christian, and a rather committed one. How could God give me a child with severe birth defects? How could God take someone like my friend, who did so much for him? Why did my mother have to die so soon?* Does that sum up your feelings?"

"Yes. Yes it does." Somehow hearing it from someone else made it all seem different.

That was exactly what I had been feeling for the past few years. When I lost my loved ones, my anger seethed, but it had nowhere to go. *Christians don't get angry,* I thought. So I bottled it and tried to be pious, saying things like, "God is in control. My daughter is now in heaven. I will one day see her again." All true, I suppose, but it did not take away the pain . . . or the anger.

"But it didn't work," Jack interjected, as if reading my thoughts. "Don't worry, nothing is secret here. That is another reason heaven is an acquired taste."

"You read my thoughts, didn't you? Ernie did the same thing."

"It is not as hard as you think. I could see it on your face first. No thought, or even a wish, can hide from us, unless we choose not to know."

"To answer your question, no, my attempts at thinking happy thoughts didn't work."

"That is why you are here. Human suffering raises almost intolerable problems. If God were good, he would wish to make his creatures perfectly happy, and if God were almighty, he would be able to do what he wished. Therefore, when his people suffer, we must conclude that God lacks either goodness, or power, or both."

"Right. If God *allowed* it, then as far as I am concerned, he *did* it. He took them away from me. All I know is that I still hurt."

"And that is a good place to start. It is also why you are here. I have much to say about this. Would you like some tea?" Suddenly a tea set appeared before us when we turned a corner in the path.

"Cream or sugar?" Jack asked.

"Both," I said, amazed that he knew there would be tea around the corner.

Jack poured some tea. It tasted so good I almost forgot what we were talking about.

"Let me tell you, first, that I was no stranger to the anger that comes from suffering when I was on Earth," Jack said. "I lost my wife to cancer, and my mother died when I was a little boy. When my mother died, all real happiness, all that was good and reliable, disappeared from my life. There would still be moments when I would have fun, or experience pleasures—what I call 'stabs of joy.' But there was no strong sense of security."

"I know what you mean. After my loved ones died, the world no longer seemed safe—good and reliable, as you put it so well. Since my mother's funeral the world has never felt stable to me."

"Quite right. All losses—friends, parents, children— have the same thing in common. What we really miss is exactly the thing we can never get."

"Yes, I know what you mean," I interjected. "It is the simple things, the being together, that I miss the most. I think that is why holidays are so difficult—you just want to see them, watch them eat and drink and laugh. I want to see Wayne gulp a soda or watch Madison hug her stuffed animals or sit with Mom on the porch swing and talk about the weather. For five minutes—that's all I want."

Once again Jack allowed a period of silence. I started

thinking about Wayne and Madison and Mom. I felt a dull ache at the center of my chest. "The pain you are feeling," Jack said, "is the pain of loss. Your heart is crying out to have them back. This may sound harsh, but think about this, Tim, because it is a part of our healing. What sort of friend or father or child would you be if you thought so much about *your* affliction and so much less about *their* happiness?"

"What do you mean?"

"When we cry, 'Come back,' it is all for our own sake. We never stop to consider whether their return, if it were possible, would be good for *them*. We want them back in order to restore our happiness. But in truth, we could not wish anything worse for them. Having once gone through death, to come back and then, at some later date, have their dying to do all over again."

Jack's words passed through my ears and hit a deep place in my soul. I could see so clearly that a large part of my grief was really selfish. I want them to come back, to walk through the door and resume their lives, to let *me* have one more day with them. My desire was for my own happiness not theirs.

Jack knelt in front of me and said, "Tim, I know the hurt you are feeling. And I know that it will never go away completely. But when we see things in their right perspective, our pain begins to diminish."

He stood up and reached out his hand to mine. I took his strong hand and stood next to him. He pointed to a different path and motioned for us to go there. We began walking up a gentle slope, following a soft dirt path that—despite its curves—seemed to be leading somewhere, like the Yellow Brick Road. I thought about the Wizard of Oz as we walked, and it occurred to me that I was a little like all four of the characters in *The Wizard of Oz*. I needed a heart to feel love for God again, a brain to somehow understand why there is so much suffering, courage to keep going on, and perhaps most of all, like Dorothy, I was longing for home. I was hoping for something better at the end than a man behind a curtain.

As we walked, I noticed something for the first time. I was surprised I had only noticed it now. Everywhere I walked I had, as you would expect, a shadow behind me. But Jack had no shadow. I stopped and stood in amazement.

"Don't be alarmed," Jack said. "I have no shadow because I am a resident. You are still a visitor here in the Valley of the Shadow of Life. Your room is just beyond the valley. When you have let go of some things, your shadow will disappear. But you are not yet ready."

"Are you sure I will really make it to this room?"

"Oh yes, yes, my friend. Love will lead you on."

We kept on walking, and I kept on thinking. I wondered what would happen to me, but Jack's constant joy and strength were helping my fear to diminish. I was coming to believe that this place was nothing but unending goodness, and my trust of Jack was increasing with each step. When we reached a fork in the path, he stopped and turned to me.

"Tim," he smiled, "it brings my heart great joy to see you here. It has been a pleasure for me to be your guide. I have taken you through the first part, but now my work is through. It is time for me to leave."

"No! No! I am not ready for you to leave! You can't just leave me alone here!"

"You will not be alone. Others are closer than you think," he said with a wink. "You will meet many people who have come to see you. Know that this is a sacrifice of love on their part, for most of them are not from this valley; they now reside in the deeper and deeper places of heaven. They have all come here to meet with you."

"That means that you also made that same sacrifice? Why would you do that . . . for me. You didn't even *know* me?"

"I was privileged to have made a difference in your life once. It is an even greater honor to do so once again, but this time in person. The ripple effects of our acts of kindness are larger than we think. You will see that soon enough."

"Will I know who they are—like you and Ernie—or are they just going to be bright, shiny orbs dancing around in circles, as in Dante?"

"They have been transformed and given new bodies. But you will know them."

"Why would they come so far to see me?"

"To pause from one's own bliss in order to give joy to another soul is not less bliss but more. If you pay attention, you will see that as they show their love to you they will burn brighter than they were before. I have one suggestion: keep on walking, but *pay attention to the flowers,*" Jack said, and then suddenly he was gone.

"Hey!" I shouted, spinning around looking for where he had gone. "Come back!"

Alone, I debated with myself about what to do next. Should I walk on? Should I wait for him to come back? Or wait for someone else to come and find me? Then I remembered Jack's last words: "Keep on walking, but pay attention to the flowers." He had never been wrong before, and he had earned my trust, so I decided to keep walking. What else could I do?

The path continued to wind up and down and around green hills covered with sea green grass that rippled in the breeze. I started talking to myself, playing back conversations and working out problems, when I realized I had already stopped doing what he asked me to do: pay attention. So I slowed down my pace and began to notice everything.

I slowed even more, practically stopping with each step, noticing every rock and blade of grass. I turned the corner around a grove of trees and found myself standing before a giant field of sunflowers. It took my breath away.

I stood there, mesmerized by thousands of sunflowers. Like the trees I saw earlier, the flowers almost looked like people, as if they had faces and were looking right at me. I knew that sunflowers do, in fact, turn toward the sun and follow it as it courses through the sky, bending their necks from east to west. But these sunflowers were not pointing at the sun. They were all pointing their faces at me.

Ten thousand eyeless brown faces stared at me. I began to tremble before this silent audience when, slowly, they all began to turn away from me, with only the sound of their leaves brushing against one another as they turned. In a few seconds I could see only their backsides.

Then they began to turn again, but this time they were turning from back to front. The ones on the left began turning clockwise, and the ones on the right turned counterclockwise, forming a line right down the middle, as if they were bowing to someone who was walking in their midst.

The strong smell of patchouli filled the air, and then a voice of laughter broke the silence, a sound so beautiful to my ears that I dropped to my knees like a mother whose son has just come home from a faraway war. The sunflowers parted, and then he appeared.

It was my friend, Wayne Ogden.

Chapter 7

W hat are you doing up here, Timmy?" he said with a huge grin.

I got up and ran to him and embraced him, "Wayne, oh my gosh, it's you! It's you! I, I, I—I can't believe it. Oh my goodness!"

He shut me up by giving me a big bear hug, the kind I used to give him every time he came home. I looked at his face for the longest time. It was vibrant and full of energy and life—without wrinkles or bags. His long black hair was shimmering. He was wearing a pair of old blue jeans and a bright white shirt. So many emotions ran through me I felt like I was about to explode. My dear, departed friend now stood before me. I had dreamed of this moment a thousand times. I grieved his leaving every day.

"I am not as shiny as normal," Wayne said, still laughing. "I turned it down a bit so as not to overwhelm you. But believe me, I glow like crazy these days!"

Like Jack and Ernie, he was glowing, inside and out—a soft, glowing light was all around him and coming from him. I fell at his feet in awe. Wayne knelt down and put his arm around me.

"I hoped you'd be here," I said between sobs. "I was really hoping. But seeing you here, really seeing you, is more than I can take. It's so good . . . so good . . . so good! You can never imagine."

"Oh, I can imagine. I've been seeing a lot of people up here and felt the same way."

"How does it feel?" I asked.

"I don't have the words to describe it."

"Man, I miss you. Life hasn't been the same without you. You were such a good friend."

"You were a good friend too. You helped me a lot. Your faith encouraged me. There were days I began to doubt, but when I saw how you trusted in God, my own faith was strengthened."

I looked at the ground, shook my head no.

"You stink at receiving compliments, you know that?" And he was right. I have never known how to handle compliments. I am always sure that people are simply being polite.

"So just believe that, would you? Our friendship meant a lot to me. I know you can't understand it all yet. But take a walk with me. I have a lot to say."

"Nothing's changed, huh?" I said with a smirk.

When he caught that I was teasing him, a mischievous

look came over him, and he suddenly tackled me, and we careened down the hill, rolling and laughing all the way. The ground and the grass were softer than anything I had felt on Earth. We both looked at each other and laughed as hard as we could. I have really missed his laugh. It was always one of my favorite things on Earth, but it sounded even better now. There was no echo of pain in it as there had been when he was living in his mortal days.

We lay flat on our backs, laughing and catching our breath, looking up at a beautiful bluish purple sky. The sky up here seemed to be changing colors all the time, one beautiful sky after another.

"So now you know."

"Know what?"

"It didn't end there."

"What? What do you mean?"

"When my car crashed, it didn't end. That is not where my life ended. That is where it began. Remember the night you heard about my death?"

"How could I forget? It was one of the most painful moments in my life."

"When you went out into the field to be alone, to cry and yell, do you remember hearing my voice?"

"Yes, yes I did. But I thought I might have imagined it. I thought I heard your voice whisper over the sound of the wind. I thought it was you because it sounded so real. But then I also thought maybe I was just hallucinating."

"No, it was me, all right. I told the angels there were

people who needed to hear from me. When a person's pain is strong enough, it echoes through heaven. I felt your pain, and I begged God to let me communicate with you. So he let me have one sentence. When you fell to your knees and screamed out your question, 'Are you OK?' I wanted you to know that I was all right," Wayne explained.

"They were just the right words. I thought about them a thousand times: 'I am OK—I am more than OK.' Those words carried me along for those first months when everything was still numb."

"But," Wayne interjected, "they weren't enough, were they? You needed more than a sentence. I suspect that is why you are here, isn't it?"

"I suppose so," I said, looking off in the distance, when a flood of memories filled my mind. "I thought I was doing fine, but I am starting to see that the grief had really taken over. You died, and then Madison died six months later. And last year Mom died. All three of you within three years. I hate to be so self-centered, just thinking about myself, and I tried to be spiritual and pious and all that, saying things like, 'I know they are in a better place.' But the truth be told, I was really angry and then depressed. Life went from color to black and white. The little stabs of joy, as Jack put it, could not sustain me."

"Well, that's why I came. It's time for us to take a little trip together."

He motioned me to continue on the path, and we walked up a steep hill. When we reached the top, we were standing at the top of a massive canyon, with layers and layers of red and gold rock, each layer looked as thick and old as time itself. As wide as an ocean and yet as deep as mountains are high, the canyon stretched before us.

"You up for a ride?" Wayne said with a grin.

I was puzzled until he pointed to a nearby tree where two large horses were grazing in its shade. They looked tall and strong, so massive and majestic they almost seemed unreal.

"A ride? Who? You and me—on *them?*"

"That's right," he said, walking toward them.

"Where did they come from?"

"Just get on and ride. I'll explain as we go."

One of the horses was bright white and had no saddle or reins. The other was gray and white with black spots, like an Appaloosa, with a western saddle and two large saddlebags. Wayne walked up to the white horse and quickly mounted it.

"That one there is yours," he said, pointing to the Appaloosa. The horse looked at me and walked up to me like he knew me, bowed shyly, and nuzzled my left hand.

"Where are we going?"

"Relax. I'll explain as we go."

The horses were so tall there was no way I could get on. I had no idea how Wayne had done it. But just as I was shaking my head in bewilderment, my horse knelt down, and I mounted him easily. When the horse stood up, I felt like I was ten feet off of the ground. I looked over at Wayne, our horses side by side. He was smiling like a kid at his own birthday party.

A feeling of exhilaration came over me as I looked over this vast canyon, sitting atop this powerful animal. I felt like a kid at an amusement park about to ride the big roller coaster. I looked at Wayne and shook my head in amazement. I was smiling so much my face began to hurt. Wayne was such a good friend, the rare friends who you just like to be with no matter what you are doing. I would have been happy to watch paint dry with him, as long as we were together. To actually be traveling with him again was more than I could have ever dared to dream.

Wayne looked at me and said, "Are you ready?"

Chapter 8

"YOU HAVE A PRESENCE HERE, TIM. YOUR LIFE IS ALREADY KNOWN HERE."

Without another word our horses took off at a trot. The earthy smell of the horses, mixed with the aroma of patchouli, made me feel grounded.

Wayne always wore patchouli when he was on Earth. It was his trademark scent. After his best friend and roommate got married, he needed a place to live and asked us if we would mind renting out our attic apartment. He lived with us for only two years, but our friendship grew strong because of our common faith, our love for the same books, and many late-night conversations whose depth astounded me. The Bible says great friends are like iron that sharpens iron, each one making the other one sharper. Wayne was certainly that for me.

We kept trotting along. I was amazed at how such a powerful animal could be so gentle, both fierce and tender at the same time. I seemed to be able to guide it without saying a word. I wondered if this horse, like the others up here, could read my thoughts. We rode in silence as I took in the grandeur of the canyon.

"I really am OK, Tim, just like I said to you that night," Wayne said breaking the silence. "It is great up here. I really am *much* more than OK."

"You look great, and you sound great," I said.

"When I was on Earth, as you know, I was really in a lot of mental and emotional pain. That spinning rock was hard for me to live on. I just felt too much. I saw too much. I couldn't block it out."

"But that is what made you such a great songwriter. After you died, I was talking with some of your best friends, and we all agreed—if you had been mentally healthy, the world would have lost a lot of great music."

Wayne laughed. "You guys all said that? Thanks a lot! Glad to know you guys still think about me."

"We never really stop thinking about you, Wayne. But continue what you were saying."

"Well, you were right in one respect. If it weren't for the outlet of music, I would have died of heartbreak. I longed for this place everyday. I was lonely and scared and screwed up half the time. Life on Earth is so beautiful and so terrible at the same time. There were days when I would just weep. And my own sins and failures, my weaknesses and hang-ups, kept me from being truly free."

"Are you free now, Wayne?"

"Not only free. I am strong."

"But what about all the pain and suffering you went

through? Does the pain and suffering stay in our memory up here, or does it vanish?"

"It doesn't vanish. Not in the least."

"What happens to it?" I asked.

"You're riding on it."

"What?" I said, "I don't understand."

"The pain—your trials and sufferings that you have faced—that's what your horse is. Pretty amazing, huh?"

"You mean . . . this horse is . . . *my pain?*"

"You got it."

"How could my pain become a . . . a horse?"

"Second Corinthians 4:17—our afflictions on Earth are preparing for us an eternal weight of glory."

"But I am not here yet, right? I am just visiting. How could this horse be here . . . ahead of me?"

"More Bible quotations, if you don't mind. Colossians 3:3—'for you have died, and your life is hidden with Christ in God.'"

"I still don't get it. What does it mean in this case?"

"It means when you gave your life to God, when you accepted Christ, you *died* with him. The life you go on living is already being established here in heaven, *even before you get here.*"

"Even when I am still on Earth?"

"Yep. You have a presence here, Tim. Your life is already known here. There are people here that you have influenced and people here that have influenced you. But it is our pain, not our successes, that largely make us who we are. Every life is bound to have some trouble, but when we reach out to Jesus, that pain is transformed."

"Remember when Madison was born?" he went on. "Remember all those nights when you cried yourself to sleep on the cold hospital floor? The pain went really deep, but having a child with special needs didn't break you. It nearly did, but it didn't in the end. That's what your horse is made of. Let me put it simply: you are riding on your trials."

I reached down and stroked the gray mane of the Appaloosa. I fell forward and put my arms around his neck. I sat back up and asked, "Why is yours white, and mine spotted? Were your trials 'purer' than mine?"

"No, they're spotted because yours aren't over yet. On Earth our battles are a mixture of darkness and light. We see, but we don't see. Most of life is a mystery. But up here it all changes. No more seeing through a glass dimly," Wayne said, then looked at me with a grin, "Are you ready to go fast?"

"Sure," I said, and that moment Wayne raised his hands to the sky like a pair of wings spread wide. He clapped his hands, and a sound like thunder filled the sky. Both of our horses took off like they had just been let out of the gate at Churchill Downs. My horse was so perfectly balanced that I didn't even have to hold on, but I still did. Soon we were speeding down the trails of this canyon at an uncomfortable pace. My heart was racing. The horses were going so fast I thought they might lift off the ground at any moment. Within a hundred yards, they did, taking off like an airplane on a runway.

We lifted off the ground, and though the horses' hooves kept moving, they were not touching the ground. Wayne let out some kind of yell, a cross between "yee-haw" and "hallelujah," I think. I looked at Wayne and saw a look of sheer joy I had never seen on his face before. On Earth he always looked a little tired and haggard, beaten up by life. Now his face just beamed.

As we rode above the trees, they raised their branches, as if to honor us. I hadn't noticed, because I was so focused on his face, that he had never lowered his arms. When he finally did lower his arms, our horses lowered to the ground, slowing down to a smooth glide and a soft landing. They kept in perfect rhythm as we continued to trot along a meadow.

"There's so much to praise God for," Wayne said, "and that is mostly what we do up here. On Earth we do our best to conjure up ideas and images to help us praise God. We get glimpses of beauty, and we are in awe, and we praise God for a few moments. But it passes. Up here we don't just get glimpses of beauty, *we merge with it.* In heaven praise is as natural as breathing."

"Let's get a better view," he said, and lifted his hands up again. Our horses shot off again, lifted off the grass, and within moments we were flying low across a crystal blue ocean. Then, without warning, sound began to fill the air. It was like the music to a movie soundtrack, but it was a thousand times more enchanting than anything I had ever heard. I could almost reach out and touch the sound because it was so thick in the air.

"You like it?" Wayne said.

"Oh yeah, it's beautiful, the most fantastic music I have ever heard. Who is making it—and where is it coming from?"

"Just a little something I composed in honor of your visit. I never got to write a song for you on Earth, so I thought I would now."

"When did you write it?"

"Just now."

"Just now? I knew you wrote songs quickly but not like that, on the fly—literally!"

Wayne laughed and said, "What did you think we would be doing up here, Tim, sitting in rocking chairs playing dull harp music?"

"No, I just . . . wow, you mean you can just *do* that?"

"Man, I create stuff like that all the time. And it's perfect now. It's not tainted by the need to impress anyone. It's just pure praise, composed in the simple joy of creating. There's this notion that up here we all take our earthly talents and use them to please God or put on great shows for one another. We tend to think that people who are skilled on Earth come up here and impress one another—Mickey Mantle hitting home runs or Louis Armstrong playing the trumpet. It isn't like that at all. Up here you realize that your talents were not yours at all. They were gifts from God. Some of us use them well—to give glory to God, and some of us use them badly—to serve ourselves, to get rich or famous."

I let the sound continue to wash over me. I felt like I could almost smell the notes as they passed by. I knew what Wayne meant about merging with beauty. He looked so alive and happy. I had always wanted to see him fully free. He had so much music inside of him when he was on Earth, and I always thought he would burst if he couldn't get it out. Thankfully, he did, most of the time. But up here the music poured forth without restraint.

"But I don't understand—this is music, and that was your greatest earthly talent."

"On Earth, we often use our talents out of fear."

"Fear? That makes no sense to me."

"It will. Be patient."

We rode on for awhile, just enjoying the sound of the music and the beauty of the surroundings. After awhile I was wondering if the "Room of Marvels," as Jack had called it, was nearby.

"What's next?"

"You see those saddlebags on your horse?" Wayne asked.

"Yeah."

"Well, it's time we took a look inside, don't you think?"

Chapter 9

The trail we were riding on meandered to the foothills of a large mountain, where the path narrowed as it took us up the mountain. We circled around the mountain, ascending with each lap. Soon we were about halfway up the mountain when the trail broke out of the trees and into a small clearing. Huge red rocks formed a small amphitheater. Wayne halted his horse and I did likewise.

"Let's stop here for awhile," he said.

I got off my horse, who looked at me with a knowing glance, and I gently stroked his cheek. The two horses then walked to a small stream flowing down the mountain through the rocks. I walked alongside the horses and put my hand in the stream. The water was crystal clear and cool. I looked back at Wayne. He was walking to the edge of the rocks and was about to sit down. He bowed his head as if to pray, and with his back to me, I saw his head lift up to the sky. Suddenly the beautiful music began again.

Wayne was playing a hammered dulcimer with his back to me. He was facing the sky. The "stage" of the amphitheater, I then realized, was pointing *away* from the mountain, not to it.

He was playing to an invisible audience, it seemed, and as he played, the sky began to fill with shining lights, as if stars had come out during the day. At first I did not recognize what he was playing, but then the melodies became clear to me. He was playing hymns, one after another, flowing into one another as if it was one melody. I sat on a nearby rock, leaned forward, and closed my eyes as I listened. Each hymn brought back memories of times in church when I heard them played. "For the Beauty of the Earth," "It Is Well with My Soul," "Come Thou Fount of Every Blessing," "Great Is Thy Faithfulness," resounded from his dulcimer.

The sound intensified, and I looked at Wayne. It was as if I could see notes move from his heart to his hands, then through the hammers and onto the strings of the dulcimer, and in a flash, fly up to the sky. Each note hung in the air, like stars in the sky, and then turned into silver wings that danced in concert with the other notes. The colors of the canyon below us—the trees and the grass and the flower petals—combined with Wayne's music, formed a harmony of beauty and perfection and love beyond anything I had ever imagined was possible.

When he finished, loud applause billowed throughout the atmosphere. I looked at Wayne, who himself was standing and applauding. Then I realized that the heavens were not praising Wayne. They were praising God. The adoration was for the God who inspired those hymns, not the composers or the musician. Everything Wayne had said to me on Earth about music, about its real purpose, now made sense. He once told me that music was God's gift to the human race, that music wasn't necessary to sustain life (you can't eat it, and it won't keep the rain from falling on your head), but it was given to us to enhance our lives. He turned and walked back to me as I sat upon the rock. I had nothing to say; words would have ruined the moment. He sat down beside me and said, "Now, about those saddlebags . . ."

"Yeah, let's get back to that."

"Well, go get 'em, but don't open 'em just yet."

"I won't."

I walked over to my horse, untied the saddlebags, and walked back over to Wayne and sat down.

"Open up the one on the left."

I felt like a kid on Christmas morning, eagerly anticipating what was inside the package. But at the same time I had a feeling this was not going to be like getting some great present. Inside the first saddlebag was a mask, like the kind on a theater playbill, which usually comes in pairs, one laughing and one crying. But there was only one. It was white. It was neither laughing nor crying but something in between. I stared at it for a few moments and noticed that the shape of the face was exactly like mine. I ran my finger across it and up and down the nose, and then I realized it was a mask of my face.

"What? What is this all about? This won't help me—unless I am going to some Halloween party. What am I supposed to do with it?"

Wayne ignored my question and said, "You have been invited to go deeper into heaven, but there are parts of you that cannot go. There is a Room of Marvels for you to see, but it is in the high country. Where you are going that mask cannot go."

"That's fine and well. I don't even want it."

"Oh, yes you do. It is very much a part of you. Parting with it won't be easy. It has to do with your fears. Where you are going, there is no fear. Perfect love has cast it out. Fears weigh us down when we're on Earth, but they are unbearable in heaven. You will have to let it go."

"But I don't even know what's going on here. What is this mask—this mask of my face—all about? Is it one of those death masks, like the old kings had? Am I dead? I knew it. I died, and you are just now getting around to telling me!"

"Relax!" Wayne said laughing, "It's not a death mask, but it is deadly."

"Please explain."

"Well, it's a little complicated, so pay attention."

"I will. I am all ears."

"All right. In order to get into deeper heaven, you have to abandon your fears. You have to give up your restless anxieties and the self-deceiving defense mechanisms that keep you from loving freely. Ironically we are often more attached to these things than we are to our material goods, often clinging to them more desperately than we cling to our friendships, families, and most loved ones. We clutch them, and eventually they destroy us."

"But I still don't get it. What is this mask all about?"

"Ernie's mirror helped you look deeply into your shame. But you have never looked intently into your fears, Tim. Now is the time. To go any higher you will have to let go of your fears."

"You keep talking about fear. I don't have any fears, do I? Am I really afraid? And if so, what am I afraid of?"

"Your primary fear is the fear of being known. That is the mask."

"I am not afraid of being . . ." I started to say, but I knew it was a lie. I was starting to get good at stopping myself when I knew I was not telling the truth. I suppose heaven was having an effect on me.

"Don't be ashamed, Tim. You are not alone. You want people to know you on your own terms, but you are afraid to let them see the real you. You use your talent with words to control how they see you. You only let them see the mask. You created the mask to protect yourself. The mask is the way you manage what other people think of you. You let them see what you think they want to see, but they never get to see the real you."

I felt like a person who has just been exposed but is not quite ready to confess.

"You may be right," I said. I continued to look at the

mask with a kind of pity. "What am I supposed to do with it now? Can I just get rid of it?"

"Of course you can, but it won't be easy. You have learned to live with this mask, and you have grown to trust it. But you have to discard it. You are going to have to trust that the person you really are, even with your warts, is worth loving. When you voluntarily give yourself away, you will be left with nothing to lose. When you have nothing to lose, you will have nothing to hide."

"That sounded deep. What do you mean?"

"No, let me ask the questions for a minute. Are you ready?"

"Fire away."

"Don't think—just answer, OK?"

"Fair enough."

"Do you see *dependency* as something weak?"

"Yes."

"Are you afraid of being fully known by others?"

"Of course."

"Why?"

"Because . . . because, if people really knew me, they wouldn't like me?"

"So you're afraid that people won't like you, that you will be rejected and abandoned. Let me expose your fear a little further. You think, *As long as I appear strong and wise and spiritual and pure, then people will love me, and if people love me, then I will be safe and secure and happy. If they knew me, really knew me, then they would despise me.* Right?"

"I suppose I have had that train of thought run through my mind . . . a few thousand times."

"But here's the problem: God can't love a mask, and neither can the people around you. The real sham is the mask, not you. Be brave in your honesty, Tim. Don't let your shame and your unfaithfulness keep you from God; let your need for him and his faithfulness to you draw you closer to him," Wayne said, with a tenderness in his voice I had never heard before. I shifted from one leg to the other, staring at the ground.

"I know this is not easy, but I am not done asking questions. Is it more important that you appear to people as they expect you to, or is it more important to be vulnerable, honest, and open?"

"I want to appear as they expect me to appear; otherwise I will disappoint them."

"Good, Tim, that's honest. But that's also your fear talking, Tim. Can't you hear it? The fear is what is controlling you. I want you to try to trust that God can use your own honesty to redeem your mistakes and draw you closer to others."

"That may work for people like you, Wayne, but not for me. People *expect* me to be perfect. Every time I have been less than perfect, I have let them down. I have seen the disappointment on their faces. I *hate* that look."

"Told ya you had fears."

I continued to stare at the mask. It did such a good job over the years of keeping people from seeing the real me.

But if Wayne was right, it also kept people from loving me, the real me, not the mask. It kept people at a safe distance so they couldn't hurt me, but it also kept me from ever being truly loved.

"Like I said, the place you came here to see is only for people who have let go of their masks. Honors, positions, titles, popularity—these things are of no value to the person who knows how much God values them. Vanity cannot live here. But think of it this way, Tim. In reality you have nothing to lose but everything to gain."

"I don't know," I stammered. "I just don't know if I could bear to have others really know me. I forgave myself when I looked at myself in Ernie's mirror. But I just don't know if I could . . ."

"If you could . . . what?"

"If I could trust that others will love me . . . for me. I am a failure. I am supposed to be one of his faithful ones, but I can't even be faithful, completely faithful to God even for a day. I am a phony, in other words. A failure."

"Everyone who obeys Christ's command and follows him fails. We all—from Peter on—have spotty records. When we follow Jesus, we don't suddenly become angels. Everyone who follows Jesus is a flawed, selfish, shallow, cowardly person. We are 'new creations' as Paul said; we are 'jars of clay.' And Jesus knew that about us when he called us—knew it more than we ourselves knew it. Our broken- ness did not keep him from calling us."

I could not look him in the eye. Wayne's words, like the

words to his songs on Earth, had a way of hurting and heal-ing at the same time, like a medicine that stings at first but starts the process of healing.

I continued to look at the mask.

"Jack helped you get comfortable with the fact that God loves you as you are. I am trying to help you get comfortable with the truth that not only God, but all of us, loves you as you are. You can't go to the deeper regions without learning how to be vulnerable, without learning to trust."

"So, what am I supposed to do?"

"Give the mask to God. You have used your creative talents to make something out of nothing; the mask doesn't really exist; it's a fabrication. But it will only crack and crumble if you offer it as a sacrifice to God."

"How can I do that? Will you help me?"

"You have to do it yourself, and you have to do it alone. You will need to learn that you no longer need to protect yourself, or to sell yourself, to God or anyone else. You will have to lay the mask on the altar and realize that your power comes from your weakness—your dependence upon him."

Wayne pointed up at the trail that went up the moun-tain. "You have to go there alone. I can't go with you."

"Don't tell me you're leaving me. I am not ready for you to go."

"No, I will be right here. You go and do what you need to do. Look up, Tim. *There's freedom in them thar hills,*" he said with his infectious laugh as he pointed to the trail I knew I must take.

Chapter 10

"Remember why you created it."

I looked at the mask and then up the trail. It was no use trying to avoid what was now my duty, so I nodded yes to Wayne and started up the hill alone. I looked at the mask as I walked. It was so carefully made, so skillfully constructed. It allowed me to be just what people wanted me to be. It allowed me to be liked by nearly anyone I wanted to like me. In one setting it could look interesting and wise; in another setting it could appear playful or clever. Like a chameleon it would change depending on its environment. But it was now heavy in my hands and getting heavier with each step. Something inside of me longed for the honesty that comes from being fully known, so I continued up the hill. Could I really let go of the mask? Could I really live without it? People would then know me as I am, and perhaps they would reject me.

I did not know where the path led, but I trusted Wayne's promise that somewhere up on that mountain I could lose the mask. My walking turned to jogging and then to running, running so hard I could feel my lungs press into my ribs and chest, until I saw what I hoped was the top of the mountain. There was an opening in the rocky path that led to a small clearing with a huge labyrinth—one of those giant circular mazes—in the center of the clearing. There was something carved in a stone at the entrance of the labyrinth. I walked over to read it: "AUTHENTICITY" it read. I had seen labyrinths before, but I always thought they were some weird, eastern, mystical waste of time. But this one was a little different. The path through the labyrinth was made of tightly packed sand, so compact it looked like asphalt, but I noticed I left faint footprints when I walked. It also went uphill on a gentle grade, while most labyrinths I have seen were flat. About ten feet above me, at the very center, was a burning fire.

With my mask in hand, I began walking along the circle path. On the ground the word "SLOW" had been written with what looked like a finger or a stick. I stopped and took a deep breath, remembering something a wise friend once said to me: "Ruthlessly eliminate hurry from your life." This place, this "Valley of the Shadow of Life," did not follow normal time—my watch was still stopped—so why hurry?

A few feet farther another sign was scratched in the sand: "REMEMBER WHY YOU CREATED IT." I stopped and looked at my mask. *Why did I create you?* I said to myself. I closed my eyes, and a flood of memories came rushing to my consciousness: being left out as a child, the time I was scolded by a teacher, the time a girl stood me up, the day I was rejected by a group of peers I wanted to impress, the night before a big job interview when I crafted the persona I thought might help me succeed.

I looked at the mask and said, "I created you because I needed something to help me fit in, to be liked, to impress people—some people I didn't even like! I needed to be liked more than anything in the world, I suppose. I must have thought it was better to be accepted as a fake than rejected as a real person. And if they did reject me, I could tell myself that they didn't reject me, they rejected the mask. That is why I created you."

I looked up and began to walk on, even more slowly than before, and with a quieter spirit as I neared the end of the first circle. I was feeling present and awake. Then I came to another set of words written in the sand: "WHAT HAS IT COST YOU?"

Cost? I thought to myself. I had never thought about a cost. *Well,* I said to myself as I looked at the mask again, *I could use a little help with this one.* I closed my eyes again, and as before, recall was present: being at a party with lots of people but feeling absolutely alone; winning an award and wondering why it felt so empty; hearing people say, "You are great," "You are so wise"; and most painful of all, hearing the words "I love you" but thinking secretly, *You don't really know me.*

"Cost?" I asked myself again. I suppose it cost me very little by way of money or possessions, but what I lost was now clear. No matter how much I wanted to be loved, I never could accept people's love because I never allowed people to see the real me. I lost the chance of being really loved because I was scared of being rejected.

I began walking again, even more slowly than before. I was deep in thought for about an hour when I came upon one last sign in the sand. It said: "O LORD, YOU HAVE SEARCHED ME AND KNOWN ME." I recognized it. It was from Psalm 139, the first verse.

What could this mean? Then I remembered the rest of the psalm.

> You know when I sit down and when I rise up;
>> you discern my thoughts from far away.
> You search out my path and my lying down,
>> and are acquainted with all my ways.
> Even before a word is on my tongue,
>> O LORD, you know it completely.
> You hem me in, behind and before,
>> and lay your hand upon me.
> Such knowledge is too wonderful for me;
>> it is so high that I cannot attain it.

"God knows when I sit down. God knows when I rise up. God knows . . ." I said, and then a light went on. "GOD KNOWS!" I blurted out. Now the message I had already learned had become even clearer. With confidence I moved along the path. I had only taken a dozen steps when another word was written in the sand: LOVED. I stared at the word for a few minutes. *Yes,* I thought, *God does know it all. But He gets the last word, and the last word is that He knows me fully, He knows me as I am, He has searched my heart and knows it's poisons, and yet—and yet—I am loved.* My heart began to expand with this joyous thought. He knows me—the real me, the coward, the liar, the fool, the phony—and apparently he loves me. God sees the real me, without the mask, and he still loves me. Maybe—maybe—others could as well. I began to pick up the pace of my walking.

Soon I was nearing the center of the labyrinth and its burning fire. I looked again at my mask. I thought, *Well, old friend, you have no place up here. They have these mirrors, you see, so I have seen who I really am. And apparently I am loved, just as I am, without your help. So your time is up.*

I began to toss it into the fire, when suddenly the mask, which had been cold and lifeless, began to move in my hand. It turned to me and began to speak: "You cannot live without me!" it whispered, in a hideous version of my own voice. I fell back in horror, lying on the ground, holding it at arm's length.

"Hey, you can't talk!"

"You cannot live without me. You *need* me! People will reject you. People will not love you. No one will love you. They will know who you really are. If they see the real you, without my protection, they will hate you. They will know you are a fake, a phony, a coward. Once they see who you really are, they will never, ever love you. Don't put me in that fire. If you do, you will have no one to protect you! Better to have your reputation in hell than to live in shame in heaven."

"You are wrong!" I shouted at the mask. "You are dead wrong! I created you because I needed to be liked. But I don't need you anymore because I don't need to be liked. Not up here. Up here I am loved. I could feel it in Ernie's chair, and it has grown stronger each moment I have been here. No one can love a mask because you aren't real."

"No! No!" the mask shouted, but this time in a different, more sinister voice. "You cannot let me die. The face I hide, your true face, is hideous and vile, but with me you are perfect and beautiful. I will give you everything you need, everything you want."

A chill came over me as I realized that the mask was not merely my own benign creation but the voice of evil itself, speaking in a voice eerily like my own.

"I want to be loved—that is what I really want—and that won't happen until I let go of you." I rose to my feet, ran to the altar, and tossed it into the flames. The ground began to tremble like an earthquake for a few moments, and I lost my balance and fell to the ground.

When it was over, there was complete stillness and silence. I stood up and brushed off my pajama pants and turned to head down the mountain. I stretched out my hands to pull up the sleeves of my black sweater. I noticed that my hands looked different. They were starting to glow. I began to run down the mountain.

I seemed to reach the amphitheater in no time, and I was eager to tell Wayne what I had seen. I suspected he probably knew it, but I wanted to tell him all the same. He was sitting alone on a rock. He looked lost in wonder. When I came into view, he turned to me and smiled.

"I never saw you look better," he said to me.

"You never saw the real me until now."

"Oh yes I did. Not often, but now and again. Your mask came off a few times on Earth. It was then, in those moments when you told me your fears and dreams, that I saw the real you. It was then, Tim, that I loved our friendship the most.

"When we are willing to be honest about our weaknesses," Wayne went on, "honest about our fears, our needs, our helplessness to save and cleanse and untangle ourselves from the webs we have woven around us, when we face them head on, call them by name, and confess them to God and to one another, we break the power they hold over us. We disarm their threats of shame, and we are filled with trust, freedom, and an understanding of who we are that the mask prevented us from seeing. And not only do we do this for ourselves, but when we are transparent, we inspire others to do so as well. We encourage them in letting them know that they are not alone in their struggles. We show them trust, and trust is an amazing thing to be shown. Remember that when you wake up."

We sat together in silence for a few minutes. "Half a saddlebag gone, one more to go," Wayne said, breaking the silence.

"Oh yeah, the other one. Do I get to see what is in that one?"

"Whenever you are ready."

Chapter 11

$\mathscr{I}$ reached in the saddlebag and pulled out what looked like a magic wand, the kind used by magicians at kids' parties.

"Wayne, you have *got* to be kidding. A magic wand?"

It was black, with chrome and white tips. I handed the wand to Wayne and asked, "What is the meaning behind this? What is it doing in my saddlebag?"

"Well, what are magic wands for?"

Looking at it I said, "I guess for doing magic. Or, pretending to."

"And what is magic?"

"Well, magic is . . . ," but I found myself at a loss for words.

"Control," Wayne explained. "This wand is just a black stick. There is no such thing as magic here in heaven. But this stick is the embodiment of your need to control your life. Just say the magic words, just wave the magic wand, and you can get what you want. The problem is that life doesn't work out the way we want it to. God just knows better than we do."

I thought about what he was saying, but I still did not understand. I had never experimented with magic or witch-craft or sorcery of any kind. Once again Wayne knew my thoughts.

"No, you never tried to be Houdini, or some carnival magician, and you never called a psychic hotline. You even made fun of fortune cookies. That is not what it means. But just as you tried to manage how others saw you, you also tried to manage God, and your life, with your *religion*. Remember what you said to God when your daughter, Madison, was born?"

Wayne had just reminded me of that terrible day, the day we were told to make a decision about how much, or how little, we wanted the doctors to do to keep her alive. How could a doctor ask a person to make a decision like that? "If you keep her alive," one doctor said, "it may just be prolonging the inevitable. You would be wise just to let her die," he said in a cold and clinical manner, as if he were a mechanic telling me I ought to scrap my car. I said to the doctor, "There is no way I will be able to tell you *not* to do everything you can to keep her alive. She is my daughter, for heaven's sake."

"I went home, went to my room, closed the door, and yelled, 'How could you!'"

"And what did you mean by that?"

"I meant, 'How could God do that to me, to us?' I

mean, I had committed my life to God, and I was try-ing—failing but always trying—to walk in his ways. I wasn't perfect, but . . ."

"Let me ask this, what if you had been perfect? Did God *owe* you a perfectly happy, pain-free life?" he asked. "A lot of us are taught to believe in some kind of religious karma: 'Do good deeds, be religious, and then God will reward you with success.' We let this idea get so deep in our souls that we try to control everything in our lives. Sometimes we even hear this lie from our pulpits. But it's an illusion. You can't control your life. True, we reap what we sow, and it's better to follow God's laws than to break them, but—listen up, Tim—you can't go deeper here unless you learn that *your life is best lived when you surrender control.*"

I thought for a few moments about what he had said. Once again, I knew he was right. Trying to control my life had brought nothing but frustration, and, besides, everyone up here was good and kind and *right.* No one had steered me wrong.

"How do I get rid of it? Do I have to go back up that mountain again?"

"No. But you are gonna have to go for a ride. Get on your horse."

I was not sure what he wanted or where we were going, but just as I was about to mount my horse, Wayne stopped me and said, "Nope. Not that way. You have to ride back-ward."

"What? How am I going to ride *backward?* I won't be

able to. . . . OK, I'll shut up and listen. I trust you, Wayne."

"By riding backward you won't be able to see where you are going. You will know you have surrendered control when you can do that with *joy*," Wayne explained.

Then he said what I had feared he would say, but I also sensed it, too, was a part of the lesson, a part of losing the wand. "You are going to have to go alone."

"No, no, c'mon Wayne. Jack did this to me too. You guys seem to leave me in the midst of confusion. I am seeing a pattern here with you heavenly beings."

"Trust God, Tim," he said, and with a smile and a laugh he and his white horse took off and flew right off the mountain. I yelled, "Good-bye!" as he ascended, and he waved good-bye. He then raised his hands to the sky as he did before, and the air filled with beautiful music that began to fade the farther away he flew.

"Time to go," the horse suddenly said.

"What? You can talk?"

"Balaam's donkey did, so why not me?"

"Great, a horse with biblical knowledge and a sense of humor to boot! I didn't know you could talk. You were holding out on me."

"Naw, it's just that you two had a lot to talk about, so I thought one of us needed to shut up."

"A back-talking horse, no less."

"Hey, remember, you're the one sitting backward. I am the one in control, so you'd better behave."

"True, very true. I will watch myself. But then again,

what does it matter? I am just here for the ride. So tell me, where are we going?"

"Can't say," the horse said. "That's a part of the journey. You don't know where we are going, and you have no say about how long, or what will happen next—it's out of your hands. All you have to do is sit there and let me take you where you are supposed to go."

"Am I going to deeper heaven? Am I headed to the room everyone told me about?"

"Can't say."

"How about preparing for the journey—do I need to do anything to get ready? I mean, how long is it going to take?"

"There you go again, trying to manage and control. You don't need anything to prepare for this. You have all you need."

Then I remembered the wand. Wayne had told me to lose it, and so I tried to throw it away, shaking it violently, but it was stuck to my hand as if it were glued there. I tried and tried to shake it loose, but it was too attached to my hand.

"It's no use. You can't let go of it by force. It will only be released when you change from the inside."

It took me a few moments to take in the truth of what he said. Soon my mind began to drift. A dead barber, a dead author, a dead singer, and now a talking horse—which I am riding backward. I always hated riding backward on the train; it kind of made me nauseous. I was not feeling ill right then, just totally out of control.

My horse ambled along a trail that he seemed to know. I, however, was completely lost. I remembered Brother Taylor asking me to read that Bible passage. I thought about the phrase, *Let it be.* Those were Mary's famous words: "Let it be unto me," long before the Beatles got hold of it. "Let it be," I whispered to myself, over and over.

Just then the horse stopped. "Take a look around, Tim."

On each side of the path was a large mural painted beautifully into the sides of a stone cliff. On my right was a painting of Mary, and on the left was one of King Saul. The painting of Saul was of him taking his last breath on the battlefield, dying upon his own sword. It wasn't until later that I wondered how I knew who they were; I concluded that in heaven art has no need for explanation.

"Saul was the people's choice to be king, but he never surrendered his heart to God. His life was a startling reminder of how we ruin our lives when we try to run it on our own," the horse said, once again proving his biblical knowledge. Apparently "my pain" has become educated in heaven.

The portrait of Mary was one of her kneeling before the angel Gabriel. She looked so serene and humble and joyful. "She chose to accept God's call, to surrender her fears, and to let God do whatever he chose. 'Let it be unto me,' she said. And for that faith, for her willingness to surrender, every generation has called her blessed," he explained again.

The horse remained between these two large panels, a clear contrast, and an obvious visual aid to help me see the blessing of surrender versus the cursing of control. I started thinking about Mary and her decision to accept what God was asking of her, even if it cost her everything. She was able to let go of the future, of the need to control, of the need to have things her way. Let it be.

"I am not Mary, and I do not have that kind of faith," I said as I looked down at the magic wand, my reminder of my need to control my world. I glanced over at the portrait of Saul, a visual image of what happens when we defy God. I tried again to shake off the wand but to no avail. I gazed at the portrait of Mary and wished I had her faith. "Help me, Lord," I prayed to myself. I looked once again at the wand.

"I wonder if it even works?"

"Nope," said the horse. "It is just a fake. But if people believe it works, then they will use it anyway."

"I understand. . . . What should I call you?"

"I don't have a name, but I was born out of your trials, your pain."

"All right, then I shall call you Travail. That's a pretty cool name for a horse, don't you think?"

"That wouldn't be right."

"Why?"

"Because I am no longer your trials. Not up here. Up here your mourning has been turned into laughter. I am a part of your eternal weight of glory."

"OK. I see. So you are now my laughter. I got it! I shall

call you Isaac, which means 'laughter' in Hebrew. How about Ike for short?"

"Not bad. Not bad."

"Well, Ike, is there any way I can hasten the loss of this wand? It appears to be pretty well stuck to my hand, and it isn't getting any looser. This could be a long ride."

"There's someone just ahead who might be able to help," Ike said.

"Who? Where?" I said, because I couldn't see in front of us. I tried to turn around but found that I couldn't.

"Be patient, Tim."

So I took a deep breath and waited. We walked for what seemed about a mile or so, and suddenly Ike stopped.

"Why are we stopping?"

"There's someone here to see you."

"Where?" I asked, and then I looked to my left, and there she was.

Chapter 12

"THERE IS MORE GRACE THAN YOU CAN IMAGINE."

*B*lood of mine," she called out to me, "Speak that I may hear your voice."

I stuttered and then said, "Who are you?"

"Hello, Tim. My name is Celia."

She began to emanate a great light at the sound of my voice, which seemed to fill her with joy.

"He turned my sorrow into joy as well," she said while standing on the ground beneath Ike. She had a large jaw and narrow eyes that were kind but looked as if they had once been sad. She was dressed in a dark blue gown. She was plain, not pretty. She had high cheekbones, a thin nose, and long brown hair. She looked like someone I knew, but I could not place her.

"Excuse me, but . . . who are you?" I asked.

"I am your great-grandmother."

"But, I, uh?" I fell off of my horse and landed hard on my elbow. Lying on my back, I began crawling away from her in fear. Up to this point, everyone I had met was a dear person, someone I once knew (Ernie), knew and loved (Wayne), or felt like I knew (Jack). I never knew my great-grandmother. I didn't even know her name until a few years ago. Growing up, all I knew was that my grandfather, Harry, had been raised in an orphanage. Throughout my life I never knew why. Though it seems strange to me now, I never even thought to inquire. There were some terrible secrets in our family that no one talked about. My own father knew nothing about his paternal grandmother except her name. But then one day he decided to do a little geneal-ogy work to find out about her. He went to the library in her hometown in Indiana and, for a fee, was told he would be sent whatever they could find.

I remember the day the brown envelope arrived in the mail. I didn't know what it was, and I opened it accidentally. There was a photocopy of the front page of the *Richmond Palladium,* dated May 14, 1913. The headline read,

SUCCUMBS 18 HOURS AFTER TAKING ACID
Mrs. Warren Hudson, Aged 33,
Drank Poison Yesterday Afternoon
Died Late This Morning

In bold letters beneath were these words:
THIRD MEMBER OF FAMILY
TO COMMIT SUICIDE

My body became numb when I read it. Suicide, madness, insanity—how much was hereditary? A family of suicides. What drove them to kill themselves? Fear? Despair?

"Don't be afraid of me, Tim. It's all right. I won't hurt you," she said.

"But, I . . . you . . ." I stammered.

"Yes, I know that you know about me. And your recollection is correct. I was one of the ones who committed suicide."

"But . . . how did you . . . what are you . . . ?"

"You are wondering how a person who commits suicide gets into heaven?" she said.

"Well, yeah, I mean, . . . wow. I don't know what to say."

"It's all right. I understand. There is more grace than you can imagine."

"Gosh, you gotta give me a minute. My theology has taken a beating up here. Don't get me wrong—I am glad you are here, but—"

"I made a mistake, Tim, a terrible mistake, and one with far-reaching consequences. Your grandfather, my darling Harry, and his siblings had to grow up without a mother to care for them. And my dear husband, Warren, could not raise them alone, so he worked to pay for them to live in an orphanage. It was a terrible mistake. A terrible mistake."

"Why did you do it? The paper said you drank an ounce of carbolic acid—that must have been painful. What were you thinking?"

"I was not thinking at all, Tim. I was in a deep depression. My epilepsy had gotten worse and worse, and my last pregnancy left me in ill health. My fourth child, little Vita, had been born two weeks earlier, but she was handicapped."

I twitched.

"I lost all hope. One day I went to the pharmacist to get some medicine, and I looked at the bottle of acid, and a thought ran through my mind: *I would be better off dead than alive.* I mixed it with water and drank it."

"I read the articles. You must have been a prominent person in Richmond. You made the front page," I said, slowly getting back up on my feet. She seemed less threatening—even emanating goodness—though I cannot explain how creepy this was. But then again, seeing dead people had become routine at this point.

"We were. My father, Jeremiah Binford, was a leader in the Quaker meeting," she said. "That made it all the worse for my family. I shamed them all."

"I had some terrible nightmares about you," I said. "The paper said you lingered unconscious, but in pain, for eighteen hours. But I still don't fully understand. The article said you left no note and that you had not given your relatives any reason to believe that you would end your life. You said it was a terrible mistake, but aren't you . . . ?"

"Ashamed?"

"Yes, ashamed."

"No."

"No! How could you say that? How could you not be ashamed of yourself?"

"Because I am not concerned with myself. I have died to myself. That is the way it is up here."

"But . . . you were a Christian, weren't you?"

"Of course. I came from a long line of Quakers. As so do you."

I looked at her face. It was not sad, but it was serious. She was, after all, my great-grandmother. If not for her, I would not be here. As she had just reminded me, her family line is my family line. She moved closer to me and looked right into my eyes.

"As I said, I lost all hope, Tim. And drinking that acid wasn't the worst thing I did. That was a single moment, and I was crazy when I did it. It was my despair that drove me to it, and my despair was my deeper sin. I stopped trusting in God. That is why I was allowed to see you. I am the only one who is not here to teach you anything. I am here for me. I am here to thank you and to congratulate you."

"Congratulate me? For what?"

"For trusting in God."

"When did I do that?"

"I think you know. When you and Rachel were told that the little child inside of her was deformed and would not live, you prayed and cried and yelled at God, but you never stopped trusting him."

"I nearly did."

"Nearly? I think not. You kept believing. You never

completely lost hope. And your faith and trust are spoken of up here with reverence. The saints gather to tell stories like yours in hushed tones."

"Our story? Our story? But Rachel and I . . . we . . . we didn't do anything except just try to hang on."

"And that is the great miracle, isn't it? You hung on. You didn't give up. That is why I am here to honor you. I lost hope. I gave up. But life kept going on. My little Harry grew up and married, and his son—your father—did the same. And then you were born. You are bone of my bone and flesh of my flesh. A part of me lives on in you. And for that, I am so proud."

She then smiled at me and held her arms out. Without hesitation I took her in my arms, an embrace full of reconciliation and forgiveness, knowledge and acceptance. Though we had just met, I felt as though I had known her all of my life.

"So, don't you have *anything* to teach me, like everyone else?" I said at last.

"No. God promised me that one day I would be able to meet one of my own kin, one who had kept believing where I had not, and that he would let me see and touch him and speak to me a blessing. Then I will be ready to go on. And now that I have seen you and touched you, I *am* ready!"

"You need a blessing from me?"

"Yes. But I already have it. I can see it in your heart. We don't need words up here. The heart of a person is transparent and real. We see one another as God does, without masks. My hands have touched and my eyes have beheld the glory that is in you, Tim. And now I am free to dance." She looked at me and smiled and began whirling around in circles, with shafts of light shooting from her spinning body like a roman candle on the Fourth of July.

"You are most blessed, Tim. You are one for whom the gates of heaven open twice! I look forward to the day when you come to the table with us."

She began walking away, into golden fields of wheat, waving as she parted. "Live your life to the fullest. Never, never, never give up. Hope against hope!" I heard her sweet voice echo and fill the sky.

I got back on Ike—backward as was required—and said, "I am back. Take me where you will."

"Good answer," Ike said. "I think you are getting the hang of it."

"That was strange."

"Strange to you, I suppose, but not to us. Things like that happen all the time up here."

Without warning Ike lifted up his front legs and whinnied and took off like a bullet, galloping so fast I could barely hang on. The trail was a blur behind me, and he seemed to pick up speed as he went. Soon we were off the ground, flying, as I did with Wayne, and climbing higher and higher until the trail below looked like a small brown line on a green and gold piece of paper.

I knew better than to ask where we were going. I had resigned myself to letting Ike lead. A new feeling of contentment began to fill me. There was peace in not knowing but trusting. Even though this ride was more dangerous than any roller coaster I had ever ridden, I was not afraid. For the first time since I arrived, I was not in any hurry. I was just enjoying the view. Just then I remembered the magic wand, and I looked down to see it, but it was gone.

"Hey," I yelled to Ike. "What happened to the wand?"

"Celia took it when you hugged her."

"I didn't even notice it!"

"You did something for her, and she did something for you. How does it feel?" he asked.

"I don't know. Free, I guess."

"That's what we were hoping for all along."

We never stopped climbing in the air. We passed through three levels of clouds. I couldn't see in front of me, so I had no idea what lay ahead, but I sensed we were about to touch down as we began to glide. Ike's hoofs landed gently on the soft grass, and he began to trot slowly up a grassy hillside. Suddenly he stopped.

I saw a man flying on a horse come toward us. Since I was facing backward, I had a perfect view of his arrival. It was Wayne.

"Yeehaw! Hallelujah!" I hollered, "You're back!"

When his white horse landed, he said, "Well, I am not quite done helping you. There is one more thing you have to do, and then you will be ready for deeper heaven. Good thing you've got that sweater."

Chapter 13

*Y*ou can turn around now," Wayne said.

I turned facing forward, and our horses slowly ambled along a gemstone meadow. Opal and ruby colored flowers studded the emerald and jade grasses. Wayne pointed to a forest in front of us, and without even a sound or signal, our horses began to speed toward it. The trees were at least a hundred feet high and were bursting with birds flying in and around them. The colors were deeper and more vivid than before. The light around my face seemed even brighter. Our horses slowed down as we neared and then began walking slowly through them as we entered into the darker part of the forest.

"We need to go through here to get to where you need to go," Wayne said.

We weren't in the forest very long. I would have loved to stay longer. It smelled like the ground after a deep rain. I saw a bright light a few hundred feet away. As we left the forest and entered the light, I could see that there was a crystal blue river that stood right in our path. I suspected this was the main river that ran through the bottom of this huge canyon. Just to the side of the river was a huge tree with golden fruit hanging from its branches.

"What are we doing here?"

"It's time for you to get refreshed."

"You mean, I am supposed to drink from this river and eat from that tree? Am I allowed to eat and drink from this place?"

"Just as you can breathe this air, so also you can live on this food."

I took a piece of the fruit from the tree, and though I had never eaten anything that was gold, I took a huge bite. The texture of this fruit was something like a pear but even softer on my tongue. I found that not only did it satisfy my hunger; it also had an effect on all my senses. With each bite I was brought into a more complete relationship with the things around me, like a camera coming into focus. I could smell better, hear better, and felt more in harmony with everything. The song of the birds, which were only sounds before, had become lyrics. I seemed to know what they were singing. Though I cannot translate their song, it had to do with freedom and joy.

"Not bad, huh?" Wayne asked.

"It's incredible!"

"It's the food of heaven. The more you eat of it, the more at home you become here. You'll need that if you are to go on. But that's not all. You also need to drink from this river."

"You mean, just drink it? On Earth our streams are so polluted I would never . . ."

"This isn't Earth, Tim," Wayne interrupted. "Besides, this will do more than quench your thirst."

"What will it do?"

"It will make you forget."

"Forget what?"

"Sin."

"I am pretty good at it. Are you sure this will work?" I asked.

"It does, indeed, Timmy!"

"Why is this . . . ?"

"Necessary? Because sin has no place up here. There is no anger, no doubt, no fear, no pride, and no worry up here. All of those things lead to sin."

I trusted Wayne implicitly, so I knelt down to drink from the river. The water was cool and refreshing. I dunked my head in the water and drank all I could. When I came up for air, I looked back at Wayne, who was smiling.

"I don't really feel any different."

"You look different."

"What do you mean?"

"Look at your sweater."

My black sweater was now bright white. I looked at it in amazement.

"Hey, . . . what happened?"

"You're just about ready for the high country."

"High country? What does that have to do with my sweater changing colors?"

"The black in the sweater is sin. You have to leave it behind. The water cleansed you. Now you are free to enjoy what you are about to see. Let me ask a question: what are the best memories you have of your life on Earth?"

"Hmm. Good question," I said, as I began to jog my now improved memory.

"OK, here goes: kissing Rachel."

"Good start, Timothy! I am impressed."

"I'm just warming up. Things I have loved in life? Nathan's laughter. Lobster bisque. Communion. Seeing Madison fold her hands together like she was praying. Egg rolls. When my friend Steve makes me laugh so hard my sides hurt. The time my brother and I bought strawberries at a roadside stand, and they were so huge and so sweet we each ate a quart. Golfing with my friends. Hiking in the Rockies. Is that enough?"

"Can you keep going?"

"Sure. The smell of coffee when I come downstairs in the morning. My hammock in June. A hot dog at the ballpark. Playing catch with Nate. The smell of wood in my workshop. Watching Rachel light up a room. The leaves turning in New England. Sunday afternoon naps. Working out so hard I am sweating all over. A roaring fire and a good book to read. The feeling in the room on Christmas morning. When a stranger sees me and smiles. Fresh bread.

Popcorn at the movies—really buttery and bad for you!"

"Here's what is interesting to me, Tim. None of the things you mentioned were sins or even involved sin. So imagine how great it is . . . not to sin but to enjoy fully everything at the deepest level. For me, music was my great love. Remember the night we sat up late in my attic apartment and listened to Barber's Adagio for Strings and how I sobbed through it. Music always made me feel things. But now, up here, I don't just hear music, or even feel it, I blend with it."

"I don't get it? What does all that have to do with the sweater?"

"I was just trying to point out that our deepest joys have nothing whatsoever to do with sin. I've preached enough, I reckon. Let's get you on your way."

Wayne got back on his horse, and I mounted mine. The horses began walking along the riverbank until we got to the bottom of a huge canyon. I kept thinking about all that he had just said. Just looking at him now, I was certain that there is no higher joy than this place. Wayne stopped and got off of his horse.

"Why are we stopping?"

"Because I want to give you a hug before I say good-bye."

"You are leaving for good this time, aren't you?"

He nodded.

"Am I ready to see this Room of Marvels?"

"You are, my friend. It is not too far ahead."

"Thanks, Wayne, for all you have done," I said, as we embraced. "Where do I go now?"

"You are on your own for awhile. You will have to climb that canyon on foot. Up at the top is the room your heavenly Father has prepared for you. Until we meet again, God bless you, Tim."

With that simple blessing he got back on his horse and flew away. I turned to Ike and said, "I guess I have to go by myself," and he nodded yes. "Will I see you later?" I asked.

Ike cocked his head to the side as if to say, "I don't know."

"Good-bye for now, friend," I said, patting Ike on the nose. I turned and walked to the summit of the mountain-side. I was wondering if I had the strength to make it up this steep hill. At least the trail was clear enough. Like all the other paths up here, it was not straight but meandered and curved. I began climbing and had been hiking for about three miles, just over halfway up, when I heard a voice.

"We've been waiting for you."

I turned to see who had spoken to me. It was a young boy, about fifteen years old, with dark brown hair, a round face, and a wide smile. He was sitting under a tree on a rock.

"Excuse me," I said, "Uh, who are you?"

"You don't remember me? Ah, I didn't figure you would," he said with a slight East Coast accent.

I looked more deeply into his face. It was one of those awkward moments when you know you are supposed to know someone but cannot place his face or remember his name.

"That's OK," he said. "You'll catch on in a bit. Ready to hike?"

"I guess so. Are you my next companion?"

"Yep."

"Are we going to this special room?"

"Yep."

"Thank goodness! I have been waiting to see this place ever since Ernie mentioned it. So, tell me . . ."

"Tim, you need to be silent for awhile. Let's just hike and be quiet. Silence is what you need right now, to prepare you for what you're gonna see. Hey, trust me."

"Trust is my middle name these days. Well, you don't exactly have days up here, do you? You know what I mean, it is an old joke—" I was once again cut off, as he put his finger to his lips.

We walked together up the steep path that looked well-worn but not often traveled. It was too narrow to walk side by side, so he walked in front of me and I followed close behind. I kept trying to remember when I had seen his face, but it was no use.

The path was surrounded by tall grass that was as high as my waist. I noticed that all of the blades of grass were pointed toward the path, as if someone had combed it with a giant brush. As I looked closer, it appeared that the grass, like the sunflowers when Wayne appeared, were bowing before us. In my most narcissistic moments I could never have dreamed this. But somehow it was not flattering but humbling.

When the path got really steep I stopped for a moment. I turned around to see back down the mountain, and from this height I could see the whole canyon that lay below it. I could barely see the crystal blue river I drank from, at the very bottom. It shimmered. I turned back to my companion who was motioning me with his hand to keep going.

After about the fourth mile, we came to a place where the path widened. Up in front of us was a tall rock, too high to scale, but there was no way to go around it. *How are we going to get over this?* I wondered.

"You got any ideas?" my companion said.

Chapter 14

"IT WAS JUST A BASEBALL, I THOUGHT TO MYSELF."

---

*M*y companion took my hand and walked toward the rock. I pulled back and stood still. He looked at me with a smile. "I have to tell you," he said, "I used to be afraid of a lot of stuff. But now I know that there is nothing to be afraid of, even on Earth."

My bold companion walked us up to the base of the tall rock, turned to me, and folded his hands like a stirrup. I suddenly understood. I placed my foot in his hands, and he boosted me up until I could reach over the rock and pull myself over it. Once safely on top of the rock, I reached down and grabbed his hand. I pulled him up, and together we fell backward, laughing.

I got the point without him speaking. I was getting used to this stuff up here. Everything seemed to be a lesson, and this one was pretty clear: We couldn't make it over without each other. We slid down the side of the rock to the ground on the other side.

"You're getting the hang of it, aren't you, Tim?"

"I'm a slow learner, but I catch on eventually."

"This one was important for you."

"Why?"

"Because you try so hard to be independent. You think it would be best if you never had to need people. Up here everything we do involves helping others, or it's for others. By the way, look behind you."

I turned to look behind me, but I didn't see anything.

"Exactly. You don't see anything."

Then it hit me—I had lost my shadow. My shadow, the inky sign of my imperfection, the ghost of my false self that haunted, stalked, followed me everywhere. It was gone, and I didn't even miss it. I shook my head in amazement.

He laughed and then cut me off again with his finger on his lips. We started walking on the path again, but on this side of the chasm it was wide enough for two to walk side by side. We walked silently up the hill, and he reached out and held my hand.

I could see what looked like a large, white house at the top of the hill about a hundred yards away from us. I couldn't take my eyes from it. It was like seeing something from a dream you once had, and suddenly you are seeing it in real life. There was no fence around the house and no boundary markers. The house, or room, was not rectangular, as most are, but had many sides. As we got near, I could see that it was an octagon. The dirt path we had been on turned into a cobblestone walkway that led to the front door.

I turned to look down the canyon, and as I suspected, it was a beautiful view. All around the house were Russian olive trees—my favorite tree on Earth, not so much for its beauty but for its scent. Each spring when I was growing up in Colorado, the smell of Russian olive trees filled the air with the promise of summer. The scent from the trees was all around me. I turned back to the door where my companion was waiting. I walked up to him and said, "Can we go in?"

"Sure. This is your place."

"My place? I didn't know I . . ."

"In our Father's house there are many, many rooms. Jesus came to prepare this place for you. It is your room."

"What's inside?"

"Come and see."

I opened the door and went in. It was one large open room, the size of a gymnasium. It was not a place where people sleep and eat; it was more like a museum. The floors were made of a shiny hardwood. There were no chairs or any other place to sit. The walls were white, and there were windows on each of the eight sides. All along the main floor were pillars, about four feet high, and something sat atop each one. I walked over to the nearest pillar, and there was a baseball sitting on top of it. Not a new ball but clearly a used one, not beat up but with a mark or two on it. *A baseball?* I thought, *Why is that here?*

"Yankee stadium, 1983" my companion said from behind me.

"No—no way, is this the ball that . . . ?"

I turned around to see him smiling, and he walked over and picked up the ball. The moment he touched it I knew who he was.

"You were the one who . . ."

"Yep. That's me! Tommy Kowalski."

Tommy Kowalski was a young boy who worked in the dish room in the cafeteria of my graduate school. I worked there to help pay for school; Tommy was working there for real. He was living in a foster home, and he was sent to the cafeteria after school. He was mentally challenged and unable to go to a traditional public school. I always loved working with him because he was so happy.

We were very different people. I had come from a good home, had a great family, and was getting a master's degree. Tommy had been given up for adoption, never knew his parents, and had trouble in school. But we had one thing in common: we both loved the Yankees. We always talked about the Yankees. I sometimes went to games at Yankee Stadium; Tommy had never been to one, but he listened to every game on the radio. He set up a radio on his windowsill and placed two soup cans next to it to get better reception. He knew every player, and even though he had problems thinking and talking clearly, he was lucid when we talked about yesterday's game.

"What are you doing here, Tommy?"

"I died, just like all of these other people you keep meeting."

"How? When?"

"A few years ago. I was tryin' to listen to a Yankees game on the radio while I was in the bathtub, and the radio kinda fell in."

"Kinda? What do you mean, kinda?"

"Well, it fell in when I was turning up the sound. I sort of slipped. I was not too bright when I was living down there. I guess I got shortchanged on the whole brain thing! It was dumb, but hey, I went out listening to the Yanks!"

"Tommy, I am so sorry."

"You oughta know better by now than to say that. I'm a lot better off up here. But hey, it's a short life down there any way you look at it, whether you go at eighteen or eighty."

"Well, I am so glad to see you. You were always a joy. I loved to see you smile. But why are you here, I mean, here with me?"

"The ball, smart guy," he said.

He liked to call me "smart guy." It was always a strange contrast when I saw Tommy each day. I spent my days studying hard, interacting with bright students and brilliant faculty, reading dusty old books by long-dead people in the bowels of the library, and then going to the cafeteria and hanging out with Tommy, who had never read a book in his life. But the most fun I had each day was talking with Tommy.

"The ball! Is that the ball?"

"Yep. That's the one. April 12, 1985. That's the best day of my life on Earth, the day you gave me that ball—the home run ball you caught at Yankee Stadium."

The memory of that spring day unfurled in my mind. It was a day to remember. The smell of Yankee Stadium—hot dogs and cigar smoke and freshly cut grass—all came forth in my mind as if it were happening all over again.

"Tommy, I have something to confess. I didn't really catch it. It landed in my cup. Four guys were fighting for the ball, and it ended up in my cup! I was trying to buy a hot dog when the batter hit that ball. All I remember is that I never got the dog, and the three bucks I was holding out for the concession guy disappeared in the dog pile. But I did get the ball, just not in a glamorous way."

"I know. The angels have a real sense of humor, eh?" he said with a giggle.

"You mean . . . ?"

"Yeah. They had it all worked out. Sometimes we entertain 'em unawares, y'know. They carried out his plan. They knew how much I loved the Yanks, and they heard all of my prayers that one day I could go to a game and catch a ball. Well, that was never going to happen. But they knew you were going, so they arranged it."

"That's amazing. But how did they know I would give it to you? I mean, I should tell you, Tommy, I almost didn't. I was so proud of that ball. It was a lifelong dream to go to a game and catch a ball in Yankee Stadium. Giving you that ball . . ."

"Was one of the hardest things you ever did, right?"

"Right."

"Yeah, they knew that too. But they knew you would. It

was your opportunity to do something that would last. That is what this place is all about."

"Yeah, speaking of which, what is this place all about?"

"This is the Room of Marvels," he said.

"I have been hearing that phrase a lot. What does it mean?"

"It's full of marvels."

"Very funny. What are the marvels?"

"All of the ways you touched other people's lives."

"What do you mean?"

"On Earth, each day we have a chance to have an impact on others. And this room is full of the souvenirs of your love, of the things you did for other people, small or great. Up here they're all great."

I looked at the ball again. *It was just a baseball,* I thought to myself, but it was here, in heaven. "It was a beautiful thing you did, Tim. Your act of kindness may not have been that important to you, but to me it was the nicest thing anyone ever did. Nobody cared about me on Earth. When you gave me that ball, I knew that I must be special."

He reached out his arms and embraced me. We hugged for a long time.

"Are you going to be my guide for awhile?"

"Nope. I only got to be your bellhop. By the way, the hot dog guy who took your money without giving you your dog? He was the angel who kicked the ball into your cup."

"Really? I have heard of being touched by an angel but never *stiffed* by an angel," I said, and he burst out laughing.

I always loved his innocent laugh.

"Yeah, he stiffed ya," Tommy said. He paused and then said, "Tim, you were nice to me every day. There was only one thing you didn't do that I always wanted you to do."

"What was that? I don't remember?"

"C'mon, remember how each day I told you about my favorite game in the world, and you always said, 'Not today, Tommy, maybe some other time'?"

"Oh yeah, yeah, now I remember, you loved to play checkers! I am sorry I never played with you."

"It's OK. Now I understand. It was because of him," he said, pointing out the window. Out in the courtyard I could see a man sitting beneath an old oak tree, rubbing his chin as he stared at a checkerboard.

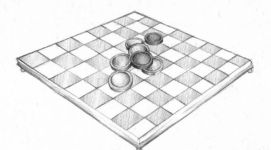

Chapter 15

It was my grandfather, Harry Hudson. He died when I was four, but I recognized him from his pictures. He had black-rimmed glasses and reddish brown hair combed straight back. He was thin, with a strong jaw and thin nose. He was sitting in a lawn chair, sipping lemonade. I stood there for a few moments, frozen in disbelief. I looked out the window at a man I knew only in my childhood. He looked so serene in front of the checkerboard, as if he had nothing but time. He loved to play checkers. Playing checkers with him was one of my only memories. After he died, I never played checkers again. It was something between me and Grandpa. He looked young and healthy, as if the strain of life had been washed off of him. He leaned back in his lawn chair and put his hands behind his head, taking in a deep breath. I could not wait any longer. I ran out the door and straight up to his chair and knelt beside it.

"Grandpa?"

"Hi, Timmy. I've been waiting for you."

"I am so glad to see you! You look great."

"Not bad for a dead guy! Say, wanna play a game?"

"Sure. You go first."

Without hesitation he made his first move, and I countered. The game moved quickly. The red and black checkers slid and hopped across the board like little round frogs. Within a few minutes my black checkers were diminishing, and his red ones were getting taller.

"Gotcha!" he said, when my last checker surrendered, and we both let out a huge laugh. He slapped his side just the way I remembered.

"You've been sad, haven't ya pal—these last few years?"

"Yeah. Yeah I have, Grandpa."

"I am so sorry about that. We hate to see our children suffer."

When he said that, it occurred to me that I really was his child, at least, his grandchild. It was like meeting Celia—someone who thought a lot about me, someone who thought of me as one of her offspring, yet someone I never really knew. He died before I got a chance to really know what he was like, his hopes and dreams. In his eyes, however, I was his grandchild, even if the last time I saw him I was a boy. Then another thought came into my mind: I recently met his mother! The man across the checkerboard was Celia's son.

"Yes, yes I was, Tim," he said, obviously knowing where my train of thought had led.

"Have you seen her?"

"Sure have."

"I met her."

"I heard. She was looking forward to it. Like she told you, she needed to hear your voice. It meant a lot to her."

"Were you angry with her, Grandpa? I mean, she left you when you were a boy. You had to grow up in an orphanage."

"No, I was never angry. Just sad. It hurts so much to grow up without a mother. Of course, you didn't have that problem. Your mother, the beautiful Rose, was dear to my heart. I loved her like my own daughter."

"She always talked about you. It is not often that people speak so highly of their in-laws, but she sure did admire you."

"It was impossible not to love your mother. She made everyone feel special. But now I want to talk about you. Actually, I want to tell you something. I know this will sound strange, but I want to tell you a story about church."

"Forgive me, Grandpa, but I was told you never went to church."

"That's what I wanted to talk to you about. You see, I did go to church for years and years. I was even a deacon at the little community church."

"But you stopped?"

"Yep."

"How come?"

"One day I was whitewashing the fence behind the church. I didn't think anyone was around, so I lit up a cigarette and took a break. Just then Anabelle Howser and Henrietta Cline came around the corner and about had a heart attack. They said, 'Harry Hudson, what in God's name is in your mouth?' I tried to put it in my pocket, but it started to catch on fire, and they ran and got some water and poured it all over me. It was so embarrassing!"

"Then what happened?"

"Well, smoking was taboo in our church, so the ladies felt led by the Lord to bring it up to the other deacons. Half of the deacons smoked secretly, just like me, but no one would stand up for me. The two women stood up and said in front of the whole congregation that next Sunday, 'Our church isn't growin' 'cause there's sin in our midst, and the Bible says the church won't prosper till the sinner is taken out. We move to have Harry Hudson de-deaconed.'"

"De-deaconed? I've never heard of that."

"Neither had I. Tell you the truth, I think they made it up."

"What did they decide?"

"They decided to make an example of me and asked me to resign."

"What a joke! You should have fought back!"

"That was not my personality, Tim. I was like you, a bit shy, and easily bruised. That was the last day I ever went to church. For ten years I had done everything for that church. I was one of the men who built it with my own hands. I loved that little church."

"That must have really hurt. I am sorry, Grandpa."

"Let's take a walk."

We walked around the grounds of this vast home. There were many gardens and courtyards. We found a bench that overlooked the canyon below us. Neither of us spoke for some time.

"This place is so gorgeous. God sure knows how to build a room."

"Oh, Timmy, God didn't build it."

"Really? Who did?"

"A whole lot of us. Jesus was in charge of the building. And what a joy it was, like those barn raisings we used to do out in the country. A lot of people pitched in."

"Wow," I said, looking around this massive building and thinking about how many people, and how many hours, it must have taken to build it.

"All for you, Tim."

"So you believed in God, Grandpa?"

"I sure did. I found faith as a boy, Tim. After my mother committed suicide, we were whisked away to an orphanage in Indianapolis. It was run by Christian people. My dad couldn't raise us on his own, and he was too depressed to remarry. He worked as a trolley car driver and sent a few dollars a month to the orphanage. Each morning we had to read the Bible and attend a chapel service, and at night we had to say our prayers before bed. There was a lady there, named Amy Carson, who had been a missionary in India. She ran the orphanage. I loved her dearly. She called me 'Dear Harry' every time she saw me. She was the most holy and pure and beautiful person I ever knew. I figured, if she believes in Jesus, then so do I."

He paused and began to smile. I had no idea my grandfather ever had any faith in anything. He never spoke about his beliefs or even church.

"I gave my life to the Lord one night in that orphanage. I was crying because I missed my mother so much, when a light appeared at the foot of my bed. I said, 'Jesus?' and a voice said, 'It is I.' I said, 'What are you doing here? Am I gonna die tonight?' He answered, 'No, not tonight, Harry. I am here because I love you, and I want you to know that. Put your faith in me, and I will turn your sadness into joy.'"

"That is a common phrase I am hearing up here."

"Yes, yes indeed, it is."

"Please continue."

"I put my faith in God that night, and from then on I became a model Christian. I turned sixteen, went south, and got a job in the mill. I met your grandmother and fell in love." He beamed as he remembered those days, and a thousand laugh lines wrinkled around his eyes.

"I left the church because I was too sensitive. I didn't know what else to do or where else to go—become a Presbyterian? Besides, your grandma loved our little church and didn't want to leave. I could have just quit smoking, or I could have exposed the other deacons, but I chose to walk away. And it was my loss."

"You left the church, but did you abandon your faith?"

"I lost my faith in the church. I let their hypocrisy ruin my love for the church."

We stared off in the distance, and I thought about how sad it was that he abandoned what was once so important to him.

"Is that why you are here? Do you have some kind of message for me, because everyone else has had some lesson to teach me?"

"Just remember this, Tim. The church is not a club for saints; it's a fellowship of sinners. All too often we shoot our own wounded because we are all pretending to be holy. But I suppose you learned that when you lost your mask. When you wake up, remember to stand up for the broken people, remind your church of that."

"So, is that why you came to see me, Grandpa?" I asked.

"Not really. I just wanted to play checkers!" he said, and we both chuckled. "But seriously, I wanted to see you and to have you see me."

"Why?"

"Because I love you. And because, like Celia, I wanted to show you that heaven is big enough to include people that don't fit the mold. I didn't go to church, but I loved Jesus, and I loved people, and I treated them with kindness. Just remember this, Tim. God's love is greater than we could ever imagine or dream."

"I am so glad I got to see you, Tim."

"Me, too, Grandpa."

"Time for me to go. Let's go inside, shall we?"

We walked back into the Room of Marvels, and I followed him over to one of the pillars.

"It is my privilege to introduce you to your next guest. Look here," he said, pointing to a piece of paper on top of a pillar. I walked over to it and saw a drawing. I recognized it right away.

Chapter 16

"DON'T UNDERESTIMATE THE POWER OF KINDNESS, TIM."

On the pillar lay a cream-colored piece of construction paper, the kind you use in grade school for cutting and pasting. It was folded in half to form a greeting card. Above and below a hand-traced turkey, written in red crayon, in the scrawled handwriting of a child, were the words "Happy Thanksgiving." I opened up the card and read, "I am thankful for you—you are the best mom in the world. You take care of me every day, and I will love you forever." At the bottom it was signed, MIT.

When I saw the MIT, my suspicion was confirmed. It was a Thanksgiving card I had given to my mom when I was in the first grade. I had a slight dyslexia problem. I spelled my name backward until I was seven.

"What's it doing up here?"

"Because it was one of the nicest things anyone ever did for me," a voice said from behind me, "and I have treasured it ever since."

I turned to see my mother, Rose Hudson. She looked sunny and strong, so different from the last time I saw her.

"Mom! Mom!" I ran to her. She stood still, opening her arms to me, with a beaming smile on her face. We embraced, and I held her tight, squeezing so hard I lifted her off the ground.

"You are still tiny," I said to her. I gave her the nickname "Tiny" because she was so petite. She smiled as if to say she understood the double meaning of my words.

"Yes, but I am still tough," she said, flexing her arm to show off her biceps, another funny thing she would do when she lived on Earth.

"You are certainly that, Mom! It is so good to see you. I have really missed you. Not a day has gone by that I don't think about you."

"I know, sweetie, I know. I know all of you do, especially your dad. I miss him so. But you just put your mind at rest now. I am doing fine. You be sure and tell your dad that! He doesn't believe in heaven, and that is why he is so sad. But maybe he will one day. No need to worry about me or even to miss me. I am right here in heaven where you knew I would be."

"Yeah, but seeing you here helps. It's weird; when someone you love dies, you just can't seem to go on because that person was so much a part of your life."

"Think of it like this: I just went on a long trip—like going to Tahiti—where there are no phones, and you can't reach me or talk to me, but I am having a ball, and you all will soon catch up, and we'll all be together again," she said.

"I like that. You are so pretty, Mom—you always were—but it is so good to see you looking like this. I—" I stopped myself. I was about to talk about her final days, but I didn't want to embarrass her. She had died peacefully while sitting in her favorite chair after falling asleep watching TV with my dad. She had no heartbeat for a long time, but when the EMS guys got there, they shocked her four times and pumped her full of medications and were able to get her heart pumping again.

It was too late though. She was comatose and brain-dead and would die naturally forty-eight hours later. It was the forty-eight hours I was thinking about, seeing her lying in bed, slowly trying to die. The doctors all said, "There is nothing that can be done. She is brain-dead and can't feel anything. You will just have to wait for her to die."

Those awful words haunted me: wait for her to die. The person who gave me life, who nursed even my smallest wounds, who made sure I was not only alive but well, was now dying before my eyes, and I was told I could do nothing about it. For those forty-eight hours I remembered every small scrape, every disappointment I ever had, and how she was always there, caring for me. Now I was sitting by her bed, holding her lifeless hand, waiting for her to let go of life.

"I know what you are thinking, sweetheart, and it's OK. And I know what you are feeling. You are still sad about those last forty-eight hours."

"I . . . yes, I was. I keep forgetting you know my thoughts. Yes, I really was sad about that, Mom!"

"Think about what happened. All of you—you, your dad, your sister, and your brother—got a chance to be alone with me and to say what you needed to say. I heard you. I was there. I couldn't move, but I felt your hand, and I heard your sweet words. It was beautiful. When it was time to go, the angels came and got me. But before I left that body, I got to hear your sweet voice tell me how much you love me. After that I was ready to go."

"I prayed you could hear me. I whispered in your ear how much I love you and how glad I am that you were my mom. You were the best. You just loved and loved and loved. You were so full of love I thought you were going to burst."

"It's a good thing that love counts for a lot up here!" she said smiling.

"What do you mean?" I asked.

"First Corinthians 13, Tim. I know you know that one."

"That's the chapter about love," I said.

"Right. And boy, God sure loves it when we love one another, and it covers a multitude of sins. You will know what I mean in just a minute. I begged them to let me be the one to show you."

"Show me what?"

"An art gallery," she said, and as she did, she pointed to one of the walls. "Come with me." We walked to the nearest wall.

"When I first came in here, the walls were white, weren't they?"

"Yes, so as not to distract you. But now you can see what is on them."

As we walked closer to the wall, I could see that there were hundreds of one-inch picture frames with photos of faces inside them. It was kind of like a yearbook, cut out and framed and attached to the wall. There were so many of them.

As I looked up, I could see that they reached to the ceiling and covered seven of the eight walls. One wall was completely blank. I reached out my hand to touch one of the one-inch picture frames, and it lit up. The blank wall became a kind of movie screen, and a film started playing. It was my hometown.

"What is going on, Mom?"

"This is going to be a great movie—just sit back and enjoy."

"What is it about?"

"Just hush, and watch, Baby Doll."

In the film a group of kids were playing in my elementary schoolyard, and a bully was picking on this shy, nerdy kid. Suddenly I—well, a ten-year-old me—appeared on the screen. I walked up to the kid and said, "Leave him alone." The bully said no way, and then I got between him and the nerdy kid, and the bully shoved me, and then I punched him right in the nose and sent him running away crying. The screen dimmed.

"Mom, I just punched a kid. Isn't that a sin? Is this another sin lesson?"

"No, don't you see? You saved that little guy who couldn't defend himself. Just hush and watch."

The screen lit up again. The face of a grown man appeared on the screen, just his face, looking right at me. I did not recognize him at all.

"Hi, Tim," the man said. "My name is Mike Saunders. I prerecorded this message for you in the hopes that one day I could thank you. I am the guy you protected in that scene you just saw. I just want you to know how much that meant to me. That kid had been picking on me for two years. I dreaded going to school. After that day he never picked on me again, and I was so happy! We went to different junior high schools, and I never saw you again. But hey, I was always grateful to you for that day. You did a good thing for me. Thanks. I died last year but not before becoming a doctor and working as a medical missionary. I died in the mission field of complications from malaria. But before I died, I helped save the lives of hundreds of kids. Come by my room sometime, and I will tell you all about it. Thanks again. You will never know how much you meant to me." He smiled and waved good-bye, and the wall reappeared.

"Whoa, Mom, that was incredible! I don't even remember that day, helping that kid." I shook my head in disbelief and walked to the walls again. "Look at these walls. They're full of little pictures like that last one! Do they all make . . . movies?"

"They sure do, sweetheart! Try another."

I went over and randomly touched another one-inch picture frame, and the blank wall became a theater screen once again. The next scene was at the annual carnival in my hometown. Now I was about fifteen. I was shooting a basketball at a booth trying to win a prize—a huge, stuffed St. Bernard. I swished five in a row and got the grand prize. A large crowd had stopped to watch me do it, and a little girl reached out and tugged on my sleeve. She said, "Could you please do that for me?" as she held out a dollar bill.

"Sure," I said. I slapped down the dollar, and the attendant handed me the ball. Swish. I looked at her, and she was smiling. Swish again. And again. And again. I looked at her, and she was jumping up and down, "One more, one more!" she was yelling.

I bounced the ball three times (my routine) and shot the ball with perfect spin, but it landed an inch too long and careened off the rim. I threw my hands up in the air in utter disgust. So close! I turned to the little girl, knelt down, and said, "I am sorry." She said, "It's OK. You tried hard." She and her mom walked away. I stood there feeling like a heel.

I was determined to get her that big stuffed animal, so I reached in my pocket and pulled out a dollar. I made three shots, then missed. I had only two dollars left, and I needed the money to pay for the bus to get home, a four-mile walk. I pulled out another dollar and made two shots before missing. My last dollar. This time I made four before missing on the last one.

The movie continued: I looked at the dog I had already won, the one that I had planned on giving to my girlfriend—my first girlfriend—who gave me my first kiss on a rainy day on her doorstep. I stood still for a few minutes, when suddenly a smile came over my face. I took off running to find the little girl and her mom. I found her a few minutes later by the carousel, and I walked up and said, "Here, take this. I won it for you." Her eyes lit up, and she said, "Mommy, Mommy, look what he won for me." The next scene was of me walking home in the dark, but a close up of my face showed me smiling all the way.

I looked over at Mom, and she was crying. "Isn't that beautiful?"

"Hi, Tim," a woman said, whose face now appeared on the screen. "My name is Debbie Kraus, and I was the little girl you just saw. What you didn't know, and couldn't have known, was that my dad had died three months before that carnival. My mom was really lonely and scared. I slept with her every night after he died—that is, until the day you gave me that big stuffed animal. I named him Scout, and I slept with him every night until I left home for college. It may have been nothing to you, but it meant a lot to me. Thanks, Tim. Let's shoot some baskets when you come to stay." She winked and then said, "Till then, take a look on top of one of those pillars. Scout may be a little grimy from all of the years and the tears, but he still looks pretty good." She waved good-bye, and the wall reappeared.

I looked over at one of the pillars, and on it stood a

stuffed St. Bernard. I walked over to it and picked it up. I ran my fingers across the soft nose and laughed when I noticed the ridiculous red plastic barrel around his neck.

"How are you feeling, Dear?" Rose asked.

"I don't know what to say, Mom. I am just thinking about how both of those things are long forgotten. Same with Tommy's baseball. I guess I did a good deed or two."

"A good deed or two? Honey, these movies go on for days. There are things you didn't even know were good—little acts of kindness that turned people's lives around, people who heard you speak and turned their lives over to God, people who read your books and found hope—oh, it goes on and on."

She turned to me, held my face in her hands, and in a stern but loving voice said, "Don't underestimate the power of kindness, Tim. I know you were ashamed when you looked into Ernie's mirror. We are all ashamed when we see ourselves as we truly are. It humbles us, it gives us perspective, but it doesn't tell the whole truth about us. We are more than our failures, more than our imperfections and faults."

She let go of my face and smiled and said, "Let me ask you this. And be honest. What was my biggest fault on Earth—my largest weakness?"

"Mom, that's kind of unfair—"

"Now you just hush and answer the question. I am in heaven, Tim. You can't hurt my feelings."

"OK. Well, . . . I think you were kind of . . . kind of a perfectionist."

"You got that right! I was so darn nervous all of the time, always wanting to be perfect and have everything be perfect and look perfect. I took the whole world on my shoulders all of the time. But guess what—I am free of that now. And do you know what did it?"

"No, what?"

"When I looked into God's mirror and saw my real self, and God reached down and said, 'I love you.' I saw that I was imperfect, just like everyone else, and it was so freeing to let go of the need to be perfect. I was able to let go of my mask, just as you did. But then I saw some of my movies, and I knew that my life was really wonderful because I got a chance to love other people."

We just looked at each other for awhile. I cannot explain how good it felt to look at her and see her doing so well. She was whole and free. "And I can't tell you how good it was to let go of that mask I wore!"

"Tell me about it! Hey, can I watch some more of these movies?"

"No, honey, not now. You will have a lot of time to see them when you return for good. Right now you have something better awaiting you. And it's time for me to go."

"Why? Please, Mom, not yet."

"I will be right here for you when you come next time. I have to go, and you have one last thing to do. But before I go, promise me one thing."

"I promise whatever it is, Mom."

"Promise me that you will stop hurting so much when

you think about me."

"But Mom," I said, "It is so hard to go on. You were . . . like the North Star for me. As long as you were alive, even if I didn't see you that often, you were always there for me. You helped me get my bearings. Since you died, the whole world has never quite been stable."

"I know, Sweetie, I know. Grief is a good thing, and when we really grieve deeply, it cleanses the wound and helps it heal. But you have grieved enough. It is time for you to grow up and stand tall. That is why you were allowed to come here. You will go back to your life on Earth with a new vision that will make you strong. Nothing can harm you now because you know how it all ends. And you also know something else: you know what really matters. It is not money or looking good or being perfect. It is about loving people as much and as deeply as you can. That's all there is, Tim. Love. In the end there is only love. So go back now and love everyone you can. Wear yourself out loving people, not worrying about what they think or your appearance or your bank account. Just love all you can."

"I will, Mom."

"And don't forget these walls!"

I turned around and looked at the walls one last time. I noticed that from a distance, the tiny one-inch pictures formed a mosaic picture of my own face. Each picture was a tile in a portrait of me, an exact replica of the face I saw in Ernie's mirror.

"We are a part of everyone we have loved, and they are a

part of us," Rose said and reached out her arms for a hug and a good-bye kiss. She gave me one last hard hug and turned to walk away.

"I must go now. I have to teach some more people how to play bridge!"

My mother was a life master in duplicate bridge, and she played in tournaments around the country when she was on Earth.

"Is that right? So who are you teaching today?"

"Some fellow named Leonardo. Apparently they didn't have the game when he was alive."

She stopped when she got to the door and turned and blew me a kiss, and the whole room filled with brilliant colors as memories of her flooded my mind. When I was six, she contracted tubercular meningitis and was one of fifty people who had it and lived at the time. I was unable to go and see her face-to-face for six months because kids couldn't be in the room. So she would lean out of her hospital window and blow me kisses. I knew when she did it just then that she had a double meaning. During those six months I would always wonder if I would ever see my mom again. Her kisses blown to me from the window were her way of telling me, "I am all right, and I will see you soon." Now, just as then, her kiss was telling me the same thing.

I was alone again. I looked out the back window, and I could see a set of stone steps that led up a hill. On top of the steps, a little girl in a yellow dress was dancing. As she walked by, Mom bent down to talk to her and then pointed to the room. The little girl then came running toward me. I knew who it was—or at least, I prayed it was who I thought it was. I ran for the door.

Chapter 17

I ran out the door looking for her. I knew it was her. I somehow just knew it.

"Madison, is that you?" I cried out as she leapt into my arms.

She looked straight into my eyes without saying a word. Her face was so bright, so brilliantly shining, that I had to cover my eyes as if I had just looked directly into the sun.

"It's me, Daddy. Look into my eyes."

I did, and I looked deeper and deeper till her blue eyes enveloped me like the sea, and I sank. I could see eternity in her eyes, and life, the essence of life. I felt a joy I had never known on Earth. A rush of memories filled my mind. I saw the face of the doctors as they told us she would die; the day she died, two years later; and how I held her in my arms, warm yet lifeless, shocked that she was gone, wondering where she went.

"It was so sad to see you cry, Daddy. It hurt me so much.

But I knew this day would come. I never lost hope. And neither did you and Mom and Nate. I can't wait to see them again!"

I stared at her for a long time without saying a word. Her face was recognizable, but she looked different. The scar from her cleft lip was gone, but her eyes were still angled downward; they were beautiful blue on Earth, but now they sparkled like sapphires. She still had tiny ears, but now they could hear. I started kissing those ears. Though she did not have perfect features, somehow—it is hard to explain—I had never seen anyone more beautiful. Her golden hair was radiant, sparkling as if it were filled with diamonds, and her smile showed no fading.

"You are so beautiful, Madison! No one is more beautiful than you right now."

"That's because God loves me. Do you want to see me dance? It is time you saw one of your prayers answered."

She got up and began dancing like no ballerina I had ever seen on Earth. She was graceful and exuberant. She leapt and danced as if life and energy were pouring out of her limbs. On Earth she was so weak, so frail, always sick and on the edge of dying. She needed oxygen to help her heart not give out too quickly, and she had bowed legs and would never be able to stand, much less walk or dance. But a friend said to me, "When you pray, just tell God what you want. Don't worry about how crazy it sounds; just imagine what you want, and tell God. Let him decide how to answer it." I had prayed, "Lord, I want to see her dance someday."

Madison stopped and looked into my eyes and said, "Well, what do you think, Daddy?"

Hearing her say the word *daddy,* hearing her speak any word, was the most exquisite thing I had ever heard. On Earth she was nearly mute, as she was profoundly deaf. She could cry, and even laugh toward the end of her time on Earth, but she never voiced any words.

"I think you are the best dancer I have ever seen!"

"I can do all of these things because God loves me and because of the love of you and Mom and Nate. I am covered with love. See, God really did answer your prayers."

"Oh, we did love you and always have. We have pictures of you throughout the house. We have never stopped thinking or talking about you."

"I know. That is why you are here."

"What . . . you mean?"

"Yes, it was me. I told God you should come to see us. He said he would let you come. I whispered in the ears of that monk, the one who gave you dinner, and told him to pray really hard that you would have the best dream ever. You were so good to me, Daddy. You and Mom did everything for me. Now I wanted to do something for you and for Mom too. You will have to tell her everything."

"I will. You can bet I will."

"And I wanted to thank you."

"You don't need to—"

"Yes, yes I do. And I need to tell you something that you don't understand."

"OK. I am listening, Sweetie."

"There was one day, after I died, that you were praying. And you began to cry when you thought about me, and about all of the pain it caused, and about how Mom was so depressed after I died, and how you couldn't fix her or your own pain or Nathan's. Do you remember that day?"

"Yes, I think I do. Go on."

"Well, I heard your prayer because God wanted me to hear it, especially the part at the end. Do you remember the last thing you thought and said out loud?"

"No."

"You said, 'Maybe it would have been better if Madison had never been born. She would not have had to suffer, Rachel would not have had to suffer or Nathan or . . . me—none of us.' And then you said out loud, 'O God, what were you thinking—it would have been better if she had never been born.' Well, that was what hurt God so much, and me too. And that is why I begged him to bring you to me."

"I didn't mean . . ."

"I know what you meant. Your heart was hurting because of all the pain I caused. But you couldn't see the good part. If you and Mom had never had me, if I had never been born, *I would not be here now.* I know it caused a lot of pain and heartache, but it was only for a short time, and now I will live forever in eternity. I would not be here if it weren't for you, and I wanted to bring you here to tell you that and to thank you for loving me through it all."

She put her arms around me as I put my face to the

ground. I was heaving with sobs, saying over and over, "I am sorry, I am so sorry, I should have never said that, I—"

"It's OK, Daddy. But now, now that you see me here, can't you see that I am so happy, and so free, and so full of joy. I will live here forever, and I will live with you and Mom and Nate forever, too, when you get here. The Bible says, 'The slight, momentary—'"

". . . afflictions do not compare to the eternal weight of glory," I said, finishing the verse from 2 Corinthians 4. "But surely it was not God's will to give us a child with handicaps. God didn't do this, right?"

"It's a mystery, Daddy. You won't be able to understand it all till you get here and see all of the rooms and one-inch pictures. But this you can trust: God is always good." She took my hand, and we walked to the front of the room and gazed out over the canyon.

"The suffering you and Mom went through with faith was a powerful witness to everyone who saw you. You have no idea how much good it did. People became better because of it. And so did you."

"I know I did. I will forever be grateful for all that you taught me, Maddie. You were the best teacher I ever had. Many years ago I read those words in the Bible: 'God's power is made perfect in weakness.' I thought about how beautiful that sounded. I even memorized it. And I thought I understood what it meant. But I really didn't."

"But you do now. You and Mom stayed up late nights with me, you worried about me, you bathed me, you rocked me and sang to me. Even though I couldn't hear the sound, I heard your hearts. Mom never left my side when I was in the hospital. I knew I was being cared for. I was held and kissed and cuddled every day of my life. Nathan smothered me with hugs so hard I thought I might break!"

Some time passed as we looked at each other in silence. Then she said, "And you prayed for me. A lot of people did."

"We did, Maddie, we did. And now, after what my mother showed me in that room, I see that loving others as Christ loves us is what matters. You changed the way I see everything. Just when I got to thinking that my career or success or my waistline were what really mattered, I looked at you. And you didn't care. You didn't care because they aren't really worth caring about in the grand scheme of life. They come and go, and they bring us no lasting happiness. The petty problems that rob us of joy, the ones that steal away so much of our lives, meant nothing to you. You brought reality home to us, and you made us laugh at ourselves. You knew what really mattered in life."

"And now *you* know it, don't you, Daddy? The only things worth seeking are treasures in heaven. And those treasures are our acts of love. People loved me, cared for me, and prayed for me—not because of what I looked like or how important I was. My weakness brought out the best in people. I asked God why so many people loved me so much, and God said, 'The most beautiful stones are the ones that have been tossed by the wind and washed by the water and polished to brilliance by life's strongest storms.' That is why, Daddy. That is why I was born."

There was a long pause until she said, "You were the best parents I could have ever asked for. You loved me, and that is all anyone could ever want. So don't ever, not once more, think of me and feel any pain. I am doing so well—as you can see! I will never stop praying for you all."

We hugged again, the kind of hug two people do when they are about to leave and don't want to go, as if their hug could hold a part of that person with them forever. I somehow knew she was about to leave.

"You're leaving now, aren't you?"

"No, Daddy, you are. It is time for you to go. But I am so glad I got to see you."

We walked back around the room and to the foot of the steps where I first saw her. As I looked at her, I understood the reason I had come. Though all of the people I had met along the way contributed to my healing, no one did more for my soul than Madison.

"I am glad too."

"Will you be sure and tell Mommy everything?"

"I will. I promise. No one loved you more than she did."

"I know. I can't wait to see her. Her room will be filled with marvelous things too. Well, I must go, and you must get back to your world. But remember this, Daddy, I love you so much, and I think of you always. Until we meet again, I thought it would be good for you to see me dance one last time. But before I go, I want to touch your heart."

She put her hand right over my heart, and when she pulled her little hand away, I felt a glow in my heart. I looked down to see that she had left a gold imprint of her hand pressed into my white sweater.

"I am right here, in your heart, until we meet again, Daddy. I love you."

She bowed like a ballerina and twirled and leapt up out the door and up the steps, bounding over each one until she reached the final step. She turned and waved good-bye and continued leaping and dancing upon invisible steps, like the angels upon Jacob's ladder. Soon she was out of sight. I kept gazing into the sky until I could no longer see her, and then I heard her little voice ring out, "I love you, Daddy. Remember how much I love you."

I stood motionless. I had just seen and heard and touched something too wonderful for me. But by the grace of God, I was allowed to see it. I was not sad that she was gone, for now I knew, I really knew, that she was well and that I would see her again. I wondered if it was time for me to return to Earth and just how I was going to get back. Just then I heard a familiar voice.

It was not really a voice at all, at least not an audible voice. It spoke to me without words, but it communicated clearly. It was the voice of God. A whirlwind swept up around me as the ground began to tremble, and a shimmering light was all around me. The glory of God was above me and then began to penetrate me, and I merged with this warm light. Then the voice said, "All is well. All is well, and all manner of things shall be well."

I whispered these words: "I am not angry with you anymore. Forgive me for not forgiving you."

Chapter 18

"Please, please, be real."

The next moment I awoke in my cell to the sound of the bell calling the monks to morning prayer. *That was some dream,* I said to myself. I took a deep breath and said silently, *Please, please, be real.* What I had just done and seen was so vivid and clear, unlike any dream I have ever had. My smile was so wide my face hurt. I couldn't stop laughing and shaking my head in disbelief. I lay in bed and thought about what had happened. I grabbed a pen and some paper and began to write everything I could remember. The train and the sweater, Ernie and Jack, Wayne and Celia, my mask and my wand, Tommy and my mother. Most of all, I wrote down all I could remember about Madison—how she looked and what she said to me.

Four hours later I put my pen down and rubbed my aching hand. I stared out my window, at the brick wall, and grinned. I looked at my watch. It was working once again. It read "1:59." I changed out of my blue pajamas into a pair of khakis and a sweater and stuffed my notebook pages into my briefcase and headed to Brother Taylor's study. He was sipping tea and looking at the river that passed by outside the window as I burst through the door without knocking.

"Brother Taylor," I said, rushing toward him, "I had a dream!"

"What happened in your dream?"

"Just read."

I handed him the notebook pages and beamed. He didn't say a word. His face looked puzzled, but he took the pages and began to read. He read them silently. I paced around the room like an expectant father. An hour later he put down the last page. For several minutes we stared at each other like two people who have just witnessed some bizarre event and have no words to explain it.

"Tim, have you ever had a dream like this before?"

"Never. Mine are the usual suspects—bits and pieces of strange events—but never one like this, so vivid and continuous. What do you think happened?"

"I don't know, Tim. The only thing I am sure of is that a few days ago a man walked into this study at the end of his rope, and today he is staring at me with a new kind of awe and wonder he probably has not had in years."

"Brother Taylor, do you think it was . . ."

"Real?"

"Yeah."

"Well, think about Joseph. His wife told him that she was going to bear a child out of wedlock. That it was God's doing. It was his right to send her away. But that night he had a dream. He saw things he needed to see. I suspect that is what has happened to you. Sometimes dreams are God's only way of reaching us. Was it true? Did it really happen? I don't know. I just know that nothing is impossible with God."

"What do I do now?" I asked.

"I suspect you need to go home. You got what you came for."

We stood and embraced.

"One day, Brother Taylor, we will meet again. And I will be one of those pictures on the wall in *your* Room of Marvels."

I took the pages and stuffed them back into my notebook and ran for my cell. I threw all of my things into my suitcase and headed for the lobby. The chubby monk was standing at the bottom of the stairs looking at me as I walked down. He didn't say a word. He bowed as I walked by. After a few paces I dropped my suitcase and rushed back to where he was standing and gave him a huge bear hug, lifting him off the ground. I set him down, and he looked at me and smiled. "Thank you," I said.

"Virginia," I shouted, "I need my keys."

She looked up from her book and over her reading glasses.

"So soon, Tim? I thought you were staying for—"

"Nope. Gotta go, Virginia. I have a family waiting for me. My wife needs to hear about a dream."

"A dream?"

"I'll tell you about it later—better yet, I will write it all out and send you a copy. You have been a blessing to me. I will never forget you or this place."

I patted my old Volvo on its roof, threw my suitcase in the backseat, and drove off into the sunlight.

Chapter 19

As soon as I got home, I ran up the stairs and into our bedroom. Rachel was sitting on the bed, looking at some baby pictures of Madison. She looked up at me and smiled.

"You're home early. It isn't Friday, is it?"

"No. I got what I needed. I had a dream, Rachel. A dream like no other dream I have ever had."

"What was it about?"

"I can explain, but it would be better if you read it. I wrote down all I could remember. Here," I said, handing her the pages from my notebook.

She read in silence while I unpacked. I lay down on the bed next to her as she was nearing the end. I heard her begin to sob. She put the last page down and looked at me with tears streaming down her cheeks.

"Is it true?"

"I . . . I don't know. It was too vivid not to be true. What do you think?"

"I think it was God's way of letting us know that the people we love and have lost are doing well. I am just glad you are home. We missed you. And I am glad you are smiling. You haven't smiled like that for years." We sat together on the bed and embraced.

Later that evening I went down into the basement to look at some of the things my loved ones left. I wanted to look at Mom's old sewing basket and Madison's bouncy seat. Most of their possessions had been boxed and put away and not opened since the funerals. I went into the basement and turned on the light. Wayne's old high-top sneakers were still hanging on the same hook where he had left them. I noticed a box I had not seen before. I knelt next to the large cardboard box and dusted off the top flaps. I could see, in my mother's handwriting, the words "Baby Things." *It must have been put here after Mom died,* I thought. I opened the box and looked inside. There were old toys, some of them mine, some Nate's, and some Madison's. With each toy I picked up, a memory came. I dug deeper in the box and pulled out a brown paper bag that said, "Tim" on it. I pulled out a little red sweater with a football on one side and "Future Champ" on the other. Next to it was a sand pail and a shovel. Inside the sand pail was a plastic bag with a note attached to it. The bag contained a lock of hair, and the note said, "Tim's first haircut."

"Ernie," I whispered.

I looked into the box and saw a small white bag with a purple bow around it. I opened it and inside was a ceramic handprint of Madison, made only a month before she died. I stared at the impression made by her small hand with tiny fingers. A tear formed in my eye, but a smile came across my face.

I pressed the handprint into my heart, and I felt a warm glow.

"Thank you."

Chapter 20

"Everything's perfect."

One Year Later . . .

It was Good Friday, and it was beautiful outside. Nathan was out of school and was riding his bike out in the driveway. I picked up the phone and dialed.

"Virginia?"

"Yes, this is Virginia."

"Hi. This is Tim Hudson. You may not remember me, but I—"

"Oh yes, Tim, I certainly remember you. The writer, correct?"

"Right. Hey, I was just wanting to know if I could speak with Brother Taylor. My wife and I are expecting a child in a few weeks, and I just wanted to let him know and to say thanks for all he did for me."

"Oh, Tim. I am so sorry. Brother Taylor passed away a few months ago."

"What? How?"

"He had cancer, as you know."

"No, I didn't know that."

"He had cancer for several years. He did all he could to fight it. He went on long walks every day, ate well, and took his medications. But it came back hard and took him fast. We miss him dearly."

"I am so stunned, Virginia. I don't know what to say. . . . No, wait. I do know what to say. I am sad that he is not here with us, and that hurt will never go away. But I know, I really know, that he is OK. That he is more than OK. And I can't wait till I see him again. His Room of Marvels will be spectacular."

"His room of . . . what?"

"Oh, sorry about that. It's a long story. Anyway, God bless you, Virginia. And God bless those hallowed walls."

"Good-bye, Tim. Be well."

I sat for a few moments staring out the window, watching Nathan ride his bike. I thought of the moment when I shouted in anger at Brother Taylor, asking him if he knew anything about being disappointed with God. I could still see Brother Taylor's face, the pained look, as he debated about whether to retaliate. He chose to minister to me, even in his pain.

I looked up at the sky and said, "God, please let me have a one-inch picture frame in his room someday. I have so much to thank him for."

I looked out the window just in time to see the mailman

give a package to Nathan. I walked toward the door.

"What is it, Nate?"

"I dunno. It's for you, Dad."

I sat down on the front steps to open the package. The return address read "J. Kowalski." Rachel called out from the upstairs window, "Tim, we need to go pretty soon. The appointment is at 2:00. Are you ready? Is Nate ready?"

"Yeah, we are, honey. Ready when you are."

"Open it, Dad," Nate said.

"OK, hold your horses."

I opened the package, and there was a baseball in it and a note that read:

> "Dear Mr. Hudson. My name is Jeannie
> Kowalski. You knew my son, Tommy. He talked a
> lot about you, and he loved this ball you gave him.
> He once told me that this ball was his favorite
> thing and that if anything ever happened to him,
> to find you and give it to you. Tommy died a few
> years ago, but we had no way to find you until I
> saw one of your books in our church library. It
> took awhile to track you down, but I finally got
> an address. I hope this is right. Again, thanks for
> being nice to my son.
>
> "Love,
> "Jeannie."

"What is it, Dad?"

"It's a baseball, Nate."

"I can see *that*. But why did someone send it to you. Is it special? Is it signed by Mickey Mantle or somebody famous?"

"No, there's no signature. But it is special. Very special."

"Can I have it, Dad?"

"It's all yours, Nate. It comes from a very good friend named Tommy. I am sure he would love for you to have it."

"Gee, thanks, Dad. You're the best. Can we play catch with it?"

"Why not?"

As we threw the ball back and forth, I thought about Tommy and Ernie and Jack. I thought about horses that fly and people I love.

Rachel came out of the house and said, "Let's go, boys."

We drove in silence for a few moments. Nathan said, "Dad gave me this really special baseball that came in the mail, Mom."

Rachel looked at me and smiled. "Tommy?" she said, looking at me.

I nodded.

"Tim, I am starting to believe it was more than a dream."

Nate sat quietly in the backseat, staring at the ball and tossing it in the air.

"Are you nervous?" Rachel asked, reaching for my hand.

"A little," I replied.

When we arrived at her doctor's office, we sat down in the waiting room.

"You know, Tim, we have to come up with a name," Rachel said. "We need to talk about it sometime. We can't keep putting it off."

"I know. I guess, after Madison, I am still so scared. I still can't believe you are pregnant. After Madison, I was sure we would never try again. Don't worry, we'll think of the right name when the time comes."

The ten-minute wait seemed an eternity. Finally a nurse called out, "Mrs. Hudson?" and we got up and went back to the sonogram room.

With Rachel's belly covered with jelly, the nurse, who did not know us or anything about us, began chatting away about the fine weather we had been having. Rachel and I were finding it hard to breathe, much less make small talk. The fuzzy screen of the monitor began to reveal a form. I could see the small hands and feet.

"Perfect hands. Perfect feet," the nurse said routinely, not knowing that our hearts were up in our throats. "There's the head and eyes and nose—all perfect. And the heart—perfect. Everything's perfect."

Rachel and I looked at each other. I loved hearing the word *perfect,* and each time she said it my joy increased.

"This baby is perfect. Do you want to know the gender?"

"Sure," Rachel said. "OK with you, Tim?"

"Sure. Why not?"

"Well, let's take a look," the nurse said. "Hmm. No mistake about it; it's a girl."

I looked at Rachel's eyes as she looked at the screen. Their sparkle had come back.

"So," the nurse said, "have you picked out a name?"

Rachel and I looked at each other and said at the very same moment, "Hope."

EPILOGUE

The most common question I am asked from people who have read this book is, "Did this really happen to you? Was this real? Did you really go to a monastery, fall asleep, have that dream, wake up, and write about it?" What they really want to know is if I really had this vivid a dream about heaven. The answer to the question they are asking is, "No." What I have written is a work of fiction.

But on another level, when someone asks me the question, "Did this happen to you?" I can answer, "Yes." That is because everything in the book is based on a real person or event in my life. That is also because I really did "see" this dream unfold each day as I was writing it. As I told my wife, Meghan, it felt at times a bit like a waking dream, or like a movie that I was watching, and each day, more of the story unfolded before me as I sat down and wrote. It was certainly real to me. Because so many people have been interested to know the story behind the story of this book, I felt like it would be a good idea to add a brief epilogue in the back of the book for this new edition.

So let me share with you the story about how this book came about. It begins with three deaths. My close friend, Rich Mullins (a Christian singer and songwriter) died in September 1997 in a car accident. The news of his death shocked me, as it did so many others. It hit me hard because Rich and I had become very close in the last seven years of his life. I lost a dear friend and a brother in Christ. It took me several months just to get re-oriented to life.

Six months later our daughter, Madeline, died at the age of two. She was born with a rare chromosomal disorder that severely limited her life, and life expectancy. She could not thrive and grow, she was profoundly deaf, and had a cleft lip. For two years my wife, Meghan, and I cared for her as best we could, and loved her with all of our heart. Madeline affected so many people in her short life, including Rich. He called Madeline his "prayer partner" and would sometimes whisper his prayers into her ears—even though she was deaf—because he believed she "had pull with God." But her little body was not able to survive all of the surgeries, and after one of them, she died. Burying a child is something unnatural for a parent to do, and the grief was overwhelming.

Not quite two years later, my mother died of heart failure. Like a lot of moms, my mother was a guiding, stabilizing force in my life. She provided strength and comfort and encouragement throughout my life. When she died, it was not so much a sense of overwhelming grief that I felt, but a sense that the world was somehow wrong—entirely and utterly wrong. I felt like a child at the playground, who looks over his shoulder to see his mom sitting on the bench and goes on playing, with the knowledge that his mother is right there with him—then suddenly the child turns and the mother is gone. Panic and fear set in. Nothing in the world seemed right after my mom died.

These three deaths had a deep effect on my soul, but I was not aware how much. Mostly I just tried to go on, to get up each day and go to work and love the family and friends I still had. Some of my friends, knowing that I had written books on the spiritual life, asked, "Are you going to write a book about grief?" I was always stunned by the question because, first, I know nothing about how to deal with grief, and two, I was still grieving myself. So I would politely say, "No."

Then one afternoon I came home to have a time of solitude and prayer and to write in my journal. I was listening to some music, praying, and writing, when suddenly I saw a place in my imagination (that place turned out to be the cottage where Tim meets Ernie). I saw the fireplace and a beautiful, serene, welcoming room. So I wrote about that room, describing it in full detail. I had no idea what had happened, but I knew that when I wrote about that cottage, and that room, I felt peace for the first time in years.

So I came home the next day and closed my eyes and saw the room. Then I allowed myself to go in. This is what I meant about having a waking dream. I just let things happen, never forcing or coercing. The peace I felt in that room was so deep, I felt like I had just had a deep tissue massage and was utterly at rest. A thought occurred to me right then: "I wonder if this is . . . heaven." It sure felt like it was. And all I could think of was about how much I wanted to stay there. But the hour or two would end, and I would return to the real world.

Each day I continued to steal away for an hour or two to go to this place and write about it. On the third day, Ernie the barber walked into the room. He started talking, and I started writing. I remember laughing at what he said, which was strange to me because one rarely laughs at one's own jokes, so it felt as if this were a real person addressing me. The character of Ernie is based on my boyhood barber, a man who always made me relax when I was tense. I suspect it was for that reason he emerged first.

The next day Jack appeared in my waking dream—the character based on C.S. Lewis. I did not at first realize this, but upon reflection it made a great deal of sense, because Lewis has had a huge impact on my understanding of the Christian faith, and especially about heaven. Lewis has been instrumental in my thinking about grief and loss, especially his books *The Problem of Pain* and *A Grief Observed.* The Lewis character gave me a chance to address hard questions about loss, and about how we can still think God is good when we suffer. Jack (which was what most of Lewis's friends called him) comes to Tim's aid and helps him answer the most challenging problems about loss and grief, just as Lewis's own books had helped me think through my pain.

After the discussions with Jack it became clear to me that the character, Tim, was in heaven, that this waking dream was a gift to me, somehow in some way, but it was all unclear. I told no one what I was doing. It was a private exercise, a spiritual exercise, and I knew in my heart it was healing me in deep places. So on and on this went, day after day, week after week. Each day for an hour or two, I would sit down, get quiet, pray, start up the dream again, and watch it unfold, like a movie running in my mind, my pen laboring to stay up with the events and conversations.

Though I never contrived or controlled what happened, I secretly wondered at some point, "Will I will see Rich? Or Mom? Or Madeline?" and desperately hoped I would. I was so thankful on the day when Jack said I was about to see someone special, and the sunflowers bowed and turned. I knew it would be Rich. Rich loved sunflowers, and one of the most enduring images I have of him on this earth is in a giant field of thousands of sunflowers.

The character named Wayne is based on Rich Mullins, whose real name is Richard Wayne Mullins, but all of his family members called him—and still call him—Wayne. After we became close friends I, too, sometimes called him Wayne, and he would usually smile when I did. After Rich died all I could think about was whether or not he was okay. Not because I doubted his salvation, but I just wanted to know he was well. I am not sure why, but that was always my enduring question. Seeing Wayne play the dulcimer with all of heaven watching answered my question.

The mask and the wand that appear in chapter 9 were not surprising to me, because many of my discussions with Rich dealt with the issues those objects represent. Like a good spiritual friend, Rich often pushed me about my need to control and impress others. The mask and the wand represent those issues for me, and after listening to a lot of readers' responses to that section of the book, I realize that I am not alone when it comes to grappling with issues of control. Rich was the kind of friend I liked doing things with—taking drives and going to movies and working alongside on some project—which made the flying horses especially healing for me. I was with my friend and we were having fun. I certainly hope heaven has flying horses.

I think the most shocking part of the dream for me was when Celia entered. She comes in a dark and foreboding way. During the entire scene in which the Tim character and Celia interact, I felt heaviness in my heart. Celia is based on a real person—my great-grandmother. My father went to Indiana to research his family tree, as they were based in Richmond. The librarian was very helpful to him, and promised to send him any newspaper clippings she could find on the members of his (and my) family. One day the mail came, and I opened a large envelope full of old news clippings. I sat with horror as I read about how my great-grandmother, from a prominent Quaker family, took her life, which stunned the whole town. I never thought much about her after that, though from time to time her face would come to mind, so dark and sad.

Right in the middle of this wonderful dream she appears, and appears to darken it entirely. And yet, within a few moments I discover why she is here. She is the first person who is there to meet *me*, who has appeared for their sakes as much as mine. It is true that she had a special needs child and, according to my grandmother, was overcome with sadness and pain because of it. This is what caused her to end her life. At least that is how the family chooses to talk about her suicide. When Celia explains that she needs to see me and hear my voice, it all becomes clear why she has appeared: she gave up, and I did not; she chose to end life, and yet her life continued on in me, for as her opening line says, "Blood of mine, speak that I may hear your voice." To be honest, as a writer, I knew it was a risk to include a "suicide" in heaven, as there are many who do not believe a person who commits suicide can go to heaven. In fact, there were some publishers who were interested in this book, but said that I would need to cut this chapter in order for them to publish it. I am glad the people at Broadman & Holman saw the importance of keeping this character in the story. Celia becomes a strong testimony to the love of God, a love that is stronger than our worst sins.

The character named Tommy is also based on a real person. I met him while I was at Yale in graduate school. I worked in the cafeteria, bussing tables and washing dishes, and many nights I worked alongside a young man who was mildly mentally handicapped, a boy from the city who was on a work exchange. He had a sweet soul and a deep love for the Yankees. I, too, love the Yankees and went to many games, and I really did catch a home run ball. When I showed it to "Tommy," his eyes grew as wide as Christmas morning. At the time, it hurt a lot, but I gave the ball to him. In looking back at my life, the moment I gave him that ball ranks as one of my better moments. I suspect that is why Tommy was the one who ushers me in the Room of Marvels, a place dedicated to the good we did in this life.

My grandfather appears next, which surprised me because I knew so little about him in this life. He died when I was only four years old, and my memories of him are dim, mostly supported by what others have told me. He and I did play checkers together. I think he appears because I needed to hear that grace abounds beyond the walls of the church. All that Henry Hudson says is exactly what my real grandfather endured. He was a good-hearted man who loved God but was judged by Christians because he smoked. Being thin-skinned, he never returned. It was also fitting that he be the one to pass me off to the next character, his daughter-in-law, whom he dearly loved.

The character named Rose was perhaps the most accurate in terms of being exactly like the real person, in this case, my mother. That is because her voice was the clearest to me. Most of the things she said were said in her exact voice, with her slight Kentucky drawl. Her words in the book spoke deeply to me while I was writing it, and it was difficult to write the sections where she spoke to me.

The only section more difficult to get through without crying was the final one, the one where I finally meet Madison.

Madison, of course, is my daughter Madeline in real life. Her life and death brought me the most profound pain, so it was fitting that her resurrected life would offer me the most ecstatic joy. When she was alive, I would often struggle with how to pray for her, so I asked my friend Dallas Willard (who kindly wrote the *Afterword* for this book, one so good it is worth the price of the book by itself) for advice. He said, "Just ask God for whatever you want. God can handle it." I told him, "I want to see her sing and dance one day." He said, "Then pray for that."

So when the character named Madison comes dancing down toward Tim, my heart broke. It was the answer to so many prayers to see her dancing. The high point of the story is also based on something that actually happened. One day while praying, I started thinking about all of the pain caused by Madeline's life (the daily chores of caring for such a special needs child, only to have her die too young, without ever having walked or talked). I actually uttered the unthinkable. I whispered, "God, maybe it would have been better if she had never been born. You could have spared us so much." I do not have many moments of revelation, and am not prone to hearing voices, but just then I heard a voice, the voice of a young girl, say, "Daddy, if I had never been born, I would not be here in heaven now." My heart melted.

When Madison teaches Tim about the real value of her life, I felt much of my grief exiting my heart. I could now see clearly how *heaven changes everything* we suffer in this life. Watching this waking dream unfold, and scribbling down everything as it came to me each day, was extremely cathartic for me. When I was finished, I typed it all up and gave it to my wife and to my father. They read it and, like me, had tears of sadness and tears of joy, and both of them told me it was healing for them. So I then let my brother and sister and close friends read it, and they said the same.

The big question was whether or not the story would mean anything to people who were not a part of our lives, who did not know these characters. I am not a fiction writer, and I knew of no other "story" quite like this. I never set out to write this book at all. I knew it was God's gift to me, but I did not know if it would be of any help to anyone else. Eventually I sent it to Kathy Helmers, my literary agent. I knew that she would tell me what, if anything, I ought to do with this story. She called back right after reading it and said, "This needs to be published. I feel certain that others will find a lot of comfort and healing in it." So we agreed to work together on it. If Kathy had not said that, this book would never have been published.

At that point the story consisted only of the dream, from the cottage to Madison. In order to be a novel of some kind, it needed a beginning and an end. So I wrote the opening part of the story, Tim going to the monastery, because my times in solitude at monasteries have been very healing. The character named Brother Taylor is modeled after a real life spiritual director I had, named Brother Madden. He really did wear jogging clothes beneath his cowl. He helped me a great deal in our conversations, and some of the basic truths he taught me continue to shape the way I see God. And as in the book, he died of cancer not many years later.

The final scene in the book is also based on real events, and is in fact an exact re-telling of our visit to have a sonogram. We really had not decided on a name for the little girl, and when the technician asked if we had chosen a name, we really did say the word "Hope" at the exact same time. I often tell people that our daughter Hope (who is now six and full of everything we prayed for in Madeline's life—she sings and dances all of the time!) is the only character in the story whose name was never changed. I changed all of the names in the second draft when the story/dream evolved into a novel.

When the process was over, I felt like Dorothy in the Wizard of Oz, when she wakes up and the dream was so real that she feels certain it really happened. That is how I feel about this book. The story was vivid and unbroken, and it healed my broken heart. I am so grateful to readers from all over who have written me cards and e-mails and letters telling me about how the book as helped them heal as well. All of us face loss, and all of us suffer the pain of losing people, but the hope of heaven heals everything.

One last story behind the story: One day we got a call from Rich Mullins telling us he was in town and wanted to stop by for a bit. We said sure. A few minutes later he and his whole band came piling into our house with their instruments. Rich told us that he had written a song for Madeline, and he wanted to play it for her. So we propped up little Madeline, who looked at Rich and the others, and he played this beautiful lullaby called simply, "Madeline's Song." He told us he wanted to put the song on a future album, but he died before that could happen.

However, he did play it in several of his final concerts, notably, one in Lufkin, Texas, which was recorded on film. The good people of Broadman & Holman (publishers of this book) were able to get a copy of Rich introducing and playing the song, and also to get permission to put it on their website. So for those who are interested in hearing it, you can go to www.RoomOfMarvels.com to hear the song for yourself. At the time of this re-release of the book (Fall 2007) it will have been seven years since my mother died and ten years since Rich and Madeline entered into glory. I miss them very much, but I know that I will see them again, and I know that they are doing well.

MAY THE HOPE OF HEAVEN HEAL YOUR
HEART AND GIVE YOU COURAGE.

JAMES BRYAN SMITH

AFTERWORD

Of all the tests that fray the confidence and nerves of Christians, the most difficult to bear is undoubtedly the death of loved ones. A legitimate part of the pain is simply *parting*. The fact that I now can no longer pick up the phone and talk to my sister or my father, or visit with them, is a lasting sorrow. But the fear and uncertainty in the face of death that is, unfortunately, the rule and not the exception is mainly based in failure of continued life beyond physical death to make any intuitive sense.

As Christians, we know—or at least have heard—the glorious words of Christ and his people about their future life in the presence of God. But, frankly, few really believe them. To *really* believe them would mean acting straightforwardly and spontaneously as if they were true. It would require being confident with every pore of our being that any friend of Jesus is far better off dead. It would be to rejoice, in the midst of our parting sorrows, over the indescribably greater well-being of our loved one who has moved on "further up and further into" the greatness of God and his world. Jesus quite reasonably said to his closest friends, "If you loved Me, you would have rejoiced, because I go to the Father; for the Father is greater than I" (John 14:28).

Jesus' attitude toward death is frankly quite cavalier. Here he is, himself, dying, and a wretched man dying along with Jesus recognizes him for who he is. The man asks Jesus to remember him when he comes into his place of power, his Kingdom. Jesus replies, "You can be sure that this very day you will be with me in Paradise." Now "paradise" was understood as a very good place to be, a place of life and fullness.

This statement goes along with Jesus' declaration in John 8 that those who receive his word will never see, never taste, death (vv. 51, 53). That is to say, they will never experience what human beings normally expect is going to happen to them. And again Jesus says at the tomb of Lazarus, "I am the resurrection and the life; he who believes in Me shall live even if he dies, and everyone who lives and believes in Me shall never die" (11:25–26). It was the shared understanding of the Christians of the first generation that Jesus in his person had *destroyed death* (Heb. 2:14–15 and 2 Tim. 1:10).

The central point of reference in all of this is Jesus, who lives on both sides of physical death: his as well as ours. "Because he lives . . . ," the song realistically sings. So Paul, rich in experience of Jesus beyond death, says confidently, "While we are at home in the body we are absent from the Lord . . . and prefer rather to be absent from the body and to be at home with the Lord" (2 Cor. 5:6–8). He had glimpsed through his own experiences the world where the dying thief had gone to meet Jesus, without benefit of resurrection.

When Paul tells the Philippians that he was "hard pressed from both directions, having the desire to depart and be with Christ, for that is very much better; and yet to remain on in the flesh is more necessary for your sake. . . . For to me, to live is Christ, and to die is gain" (1:21–24), he is expressing an unstrained, easy confidence about the continuity of his life and person that was founded on his experiences of the world of God and of the place of Jesus in it. His experiences made it *real for him,* and made it easy and natural for him to act as if Jesus and his Kingdom were the enduring reality for the enduring life of those in Jesus' care.

It is assurance of the continuity of our lives under God and in this universe with him that liberates us from the sorrow of those "who have no hope" (1 Thess. 4:13). And it is on precisely this point that James Smith's wonderful story helps us. The biblical and theological content is quite solid—though it will be surprising to many who do not put concrete content and image and action into their reading of the Bible and their theological reflection. It must be surprising if it is to address the need. And the need is great—appalling, when you observe how devout Christians suffer in the face of physical death. The reason Jesus wept at the tomb of Lazarus (John 11:35) was certainly because of the misery imposed upon humanity by failure to vividly see the reality of undying life in God—a misery overwhelmingly exemplified in the scene surrounding him at the moment.

It is also important that the treatment be with a light touch—gentle and slyly humorous. Yet, at the same time, deeply touching, intelligent, and realistic. We are all familiar with this in the writings of C. S. Lewis and others. James Smith has achieved this fine combination of qualities. As a result, you experience the writing as you would any outstanding literary work. Enjoy it. Its effects for making real through imagination the truth and reality now of life beyond physical death will take care of themselves. The "assurance of the continuity of our lives under God and in this universe with him" will creep into your soul. The Word and the Spirit will enter with the story. We are able to see the truths of Scripture in a way that grips us, strengthens us, directs us in life, and lifts the burden of pain and meaninglessness imposed upon those unable to think concretely about the course of our lives as unceasing spiritual beings in God's rich universe. Paradise is now in session.

Dallas Willard

ACKNOWLEDGEMENTS

I would like to thank:

My beautiful, loving, supportive wife, Meghan, for your unending encouragement. Thank you for providing me with a living example of how to deal with loss and grief with dignity and faith. You are one of God's greatest gifts to me.

My father, Calvin Smith, who read the very first draft, and the second and third, with lots of helpful ideas. I could not have a better dad.

My sister, Vicki Price, who gave me great feedback and lots of encouragement, as you always do.

Patrick and Janeen Sehl, for reading each draft and walking with me on this project every step of the way with tremendous support.

David Mullins, Trevor Hinz, and Ken Rawson—for encouraging me to keep writing this book, and for watching over my soul every week.

Jimmy Taylor, one of the very first to read it, for your strong assurance that this was of value.

The following dear friends and family members who read this book in its first draft and found just the right words to help me keep at it. Many of you offered helpful suggestions that found their way into the book. It is difficult to tell you how important your encouragement was, so please accept my heartfelt thanks: Andrea Price, Matt Berthot, Marcus Randall, Sheryl Wilson, Scott Price, Annette Saunders, Penny Johnson, Emil Johnson, Jennifer Jantz, Marv Hinten, Nancy Hinten, Gary and Cindy Read, Erin Casey, Robin Mullins, and Lori Gillach. Also, thanks to David Price, for staying up late and catching typos, and Megan Price, for loving the book and passing it along to others.

Jeff and Meredith Gannon—Jeff for being my pastor and spiritual friend (your sermons are echoed throughout this book) and Meredith for being so supportive of this book from the beginning. My "inklings"-like group—Chris Kettler, Charles Parker, Sheree Gerig, Lisa Hawkins, Darcy Zabel, and Michael Criss. Thank you for your careful reading and insightful advice. I could not assemble a finer group. The book would not be the same without that Saturday afternoon you spent helping me make this book better.

Darcy Zabel, for participating in this project at several stages. Thank you for your willingness to read the manuscript at three different stages, and for offering brilliant suggestions each time. Your editing skills are unsurpassed. I cannot thank you enough.

Kathryn Helmers, my agent and friend, for helping shape this book, and for your hard work to find just the right publisher. I will always remember your statement during the wait to see if anyone wanted to publish it: "The only publishing house who deserves this book is one that loves it as much as I do." Your words made me believe.

Molly Powers-Stephenson and Keith Rowley, for a very helpful critique of the second draft, offering significant insights at an important stage.

Gary Terashita, my editor at Broadman and Holman, for calling me personally and telling me how much this book meant to you, for your constant belief in it, and your relentless pursuit to see it done right. You are the best.

David Woodard and Paul Mikos, for believing in this book and working hard to make it better. I am thankful that I get to work with people like you. Your spiritual authenticity and amazing talent are a rare combination. B&H is blessed to have you both.

Anne Lamott, for your wonderful words of encouragement in your writing workshop, Word by Word (I listened to the tapes over and over) and your book, *Bird by Bird.* Your workshop and book gave me the guts to try writing something outside of my genre by convincing me that the real payoff of writing is in the act of writing itself. You have taught me a lot about the craft of writing—some of which actually entered this book (one-inch picture frames). Though I have never met you, your voice encouraged me many times. Thank you.

Chris Rice, for your music that inspired me each day as I wrote. I often started each writing session by listening to one of your CDs. Something about your voice and lyrics and music ushered me to a sacred place in my imagination.

C. S. Lewis and Dallas Willard, for the formation of my understanding of heaven. In particular, Lewis's *The*

Great Divorce, and his essay, "The Weight of Glory" are so much a part of my imagination that it is difficult to think of heaven without thinking of those two influences. Thank you, Dallas, for teaching me much about the nature and grandeur of heaven.

Ronda Magness, for constant encouragement. Christie and Tom Ridenhour, for the great pen!

Steve Nickles, for coming alongside of this project like a true friend, living it with me and making it your burden as well. Thanks for your friendship, and for your contributions to this book.

I also want to thank my son, Jacob. You were only four years old when Rich and Madeline died. More than once you reassured me, "They're in heaven, Dad. The angels came and got 'em." I am more certain than ever that you were right. Now you are a teenager, and every day you make my life wonderful. Being your dad is one of my greatest privileges.

Finally, this book would not have been written were it not for my three great stars in heaven. My soul friend Rich Mullins, my daughter Madeline, and my mother Wanda Smith. Were it not for the kind of people you were and are—so amazing I cannot fill the void you have left—this novel would not have happened. I only hope to be in your room of marvels some day.

NOTES

The title, *Room of Marvels,* was inspired by a line I read in a book called *How to Read a Poem*, by Edward Hirsch (A DoubleTakeBook, Harcourt Inc., New York). He writes, "The apologist for surrealism, Andre Breton, described poetry as 'a room of marvels'" (p. 32).

CHAPTER 2

"Begin to love as God loves, and thy grief will assuage; but for comfort wait His time. What He will do for thee, He only knows. It may be thou wilt never know what He will do, but only what He has done. It was too good for thee to know save by receiving it. The moment thou art capable of it, thine it will be." Comes from George MacDonald, from the essay "Sorrow the Pledge of Joy."

CHAPTER 5

The dialogue with Jack before the cross was inspired by the George Herbert poem *Love III*, also known as "Love Bade Me Welcome."

CHAPTER 6

"That is why you are here," Jack said. "Human suffering raises almost intolerable problems. *If God were good, He would wish to make His creatures perfectly happy, and if God were almighty, He would be able to do what He wished. Therefore, when His people suffer, we must conclude that God lacks either goodness, or power, or both.*" The text in italics is a direct quote taken from *The Problem of Pain*, C. S. Lewis, (Macmillan: New York, 1961), p. 26.

"Let me tell you, first, that I was no stranger to the anger that comes from suffering when I was on Earth," Jack said. I lost my wife to cancer and my mother died when I was a little boy. *When my mother died all real happiness, all that was good and reliable, disappeared from my life. There would still be moments when I would have fun, or experience pleasures—what I call 'stabs of joy.'* But there was no strong sense of security." The text in italics is a direct quote taken from *Surprised by Joy*, C. S. Lewis (Harcourt Brace Jovanovich: New York, 1955), p. 21.

"The pain you are feeling," Jack said, "is the pain of loss. Your heart is crying out to have them back. But think about this, Tim: *what sort of friend or father or child would you be if you thought so much about your affliction and so much less about their happiness?*"

"What do you mean?" I asked.

"*When we cry, 'Come back,' it is all for our own sake. We never stop to consider whether their return, if it were possible, would be good for them. We want them back in order to restore our happiness. But in truth, we could not wish anything worse for them. Having once got through death, to come back and then, at some later date, have their dying to do all over again."* The text in italics is a slightly modified quote taken from *A Grief Observed*, C. S. Lewis (HarperSanFrancisco: San Francisco, 1989), p. 53.

CHAPTER 18

"I asked God why so many people loved me so much, and God said, 'The most beautiful stones are the ones that have been tossed by the wind and washed by the water and polished to brilliance by life's strongest storms.'" This quote comes from an article in the *Wichita Eagle,* 12-29-01, 1F. They are words that Hans and Karen Kraus put in their Christmas letter to their friends and family.